# A THANKSGIVING FULL OF GRATITUDE

## A KATAMA BAY SERIES

### KATIE WINTERS

D1521378

# CHAPTER ONE

## TEN YEARS AGO

JANINE GRIMSON POTTER awoke on the morning of her thirty-third birthday on Rue St. Dominique in the seventh arrondissement in Paris, France, as the light cascaded through the glorious streets and illuminated her sterling white bed sheets. Someone had opened the curtains, and they fluttered out on either side of the window, presenting a near-perfect view of the Eiffel Tower just down the street. It was just like entering a dream. But Janine knew, just like everything else that had happened since she'd met Jack Potter over a decade before, that this wasn't a dream. It was very much reality—and it was perfect.

Janine lifted her torso from the overly-fluffed pillows so that her silk pajama dress glittered in the light. At the far end of the large bed, a broad tray displayed a near-perfect breakfast platter filled with buttery croissants, strawberries and raspberries, along with an array of French cheeses, sparkling orange juice, and bubbling champagne. Janine dropped her head back so that her dark curls cascaded down her back. How luxurious this all was. What did it mean to be thirty-three? To her, it meant being in love for another year; it meant raising two beautiful daughters back in Manhattan; it meant spontaneous trips to Paris.

Her thirty-third year couldn't have been further from her first eighteen years of life when Nancy Grimson had raised Janine the best she could in Brooklyn. They hadn't had two pennies to rub together. Janine hadn't been in contact with her mother in years. She had to assume it was better that way. Nancy was toxic, a mess of a human being. Janine prayed she would never resemble her.

"Is that my darling birthday girl?" Jack Potter stepped in from the balcony, where he'd stood to take in the views of the Eiffel Tower and the bustling streets below. He looked so handsome; his black hair remained thick, his muscles firm from hours at the gym, and his smile arrogant and brash, yet entirely hers, proof of their love for one another. When Jack Potter, the son of oil tycoon parents, had committed his life to her, Janine had known hers was a storybook romance, the stuff of fairytales. She'd never looked back.

"Good morning." Janine closed her eyes as he placed a kiss on her lips and smoothed her hair. "I see breakfast has arrived already?"

They sat cross-legged on the end of the bed like children, nibbling croissants and sipping champagne and practicing their best French accents. Back in Brooklyn, Janine's best friend had been Maxine Aubert, who had moved to the States from France as a child and never really lost her accent— something Jack and Janine joked she did on purpose. "It's working for her," Janine had pointed out several times, watching as Maxine social-climbed her way into her and Jack's arena.

"What do you want to do today?" Jack asked now. "You're in Paris. It's your birthday. Name what's next."

Janine desperately wanted to call her girls but knew they wouldn't be up yet, considering they were six hours ahead of New York City time. Maybe before they left for school, she would give Maggie and Alyssa a call, where they stayed with Jack's parents. Maggie was aged fourteen, and Alyssa was aged twelve, both turning into beautiful young ladies, incredibly smart and funny, at the very beginning stages of puberty and all its chaos. Both looked remarkably like Janine, with gorgeous dark brown locks and eyes the color of the deep blue sea, but their upbringing couldn't have been more different. Jack gave them the world. Education, money and social status— it had all been theirs the day they'd been conceived. Janine sometimes struggled with the fact that they could never understand what it meant to live in poverty, to feel the power of a dollar. Still, she wouldn't have traded their life for the world.

Janine and Jack showered together that morning in a large, walk-in shower, captivated with one another and lost in the warm spritz of the spray and the buzzing steam around them. After, Jack wrapped a fuzzy towel around her shoulders and placed another kiss on her forehead. In the mirror, Janine spotted the first set of wrinkles across her forehead and around her eyes. Facials. Botox. Creams. This was the early remedy for that, and these were already whispered amongst the other women in high-society Manhattan.

Janine donned a dark green silk dress, a pair of tights, and a pair of Mansur Gavriel lace-up boots, which she had purchased the previous afternoon in the Marais. She then slipped on a khaki trench, added another layer of lipstick, and gave herself a final up-down in the mirror. She caught Jack's gaze then as he finalized his own look with a whip of his jacket over his broad shoulders.

He stepped up behind her, wrapped his arms around her belly, and whispered into her ear. "You look beautiful."

"Aren't you full of compliments this morning?"

"There's more where that came from."

It was the end of March, which, in Parisian terms, meant the sparkling sunshine could fall to shadowy greys and fluttering rains in no time flat. As Janine and Jack breezed down Rue St. Dominique, Jack purchased an umbrella from a side-street retailer and snapped it up over their heads, just as the rain started. He suggested they walk to the Musee d'Orsay for a morning of Impressionist paintings, followed by a fancy lunch at Savarin la table. Janine slipped her arm through his and allowed herself to be escorted through the first hours of her thirty-third birthday, just as she'd allowed Jack to escort her through everything else in life. When she found herself before some of the splendorous paintings at Musee d'Orsay, she was nearly brought to her knees.

It had been a long time since Janine had illustrated to Jack the depths of her gratefulness for the world he had given her. She never wanted to embarrass him nor point to how little she'd had prior to their spontaneous meeting all those years ago. Over lunch, as he spoke near-perfect French to the waiter at Savarin la table, a waiter who already knew his name (such was the life of Jack Potter), her heart couldn't help but perform a funny tap-dance across her diaphragm.

"What is that look for?" Jack asked as the waiter disbanded.

Janine placed the edge of her wine glass against her bottom lip. There weren't enough words in the universe— not in French, nor

English, nor Hindi to express what he and their children meant to her.

"Just thank you," she breathed finally. "For all of this."

Jack arched a single dark eyebrow as a laugh bubbled out from his throat. "There's much more. We've barely cracked the surface of your birthday. I hope you're prepared."

As Janine wandered the rain-glazed streets of Saint-Germaine-des-Prés later that afternoon, Janine grew lost in memory: one of her mother's thirty-third birthday. As Nancy had had Janine at the age of sixteen, Janine had been nearly seventeen on Nancy's thirty-third. It was burned deep in her memory— the pancakes at the little diner down the road, her mother halfway through a bottle of wine before mid-day, her mother's whispered words, "Never trust any man on this earth." Janine had seen how other people on the streets turned their eyes away from the drunken stupor of a woman. Somehow, in the pit of her belly, she'd known that Nancy wouldn't be around much longer.

"Where did you go?" Jack asked.

Janine cleared her throat. "What do you mean?"

"You were lost in thought for a moment. What were you thinking about?"

"Oh, nothing. I was just looking in the shop windows. There are so many beautiful things to buy and so many beautiful things I don't need."

Regardless of that truth, Janine made her way through numerous shops, purchasing several items, like scarves, a Hermès belt, perfume for Maggie and skin care for Alyssa. It was times like these that she loved to pick up little gifts for her girls. Jack waited patiently, either outside the stores or in a neighboring bar, where he sipped a very small glass of Carbernet and read the Parisian paper. Once, when Janine returned from a shop to meet him, she caught several women ogling him as they passed by. Janine knew that French men were the sort to step outside of their marriages; it was culturally accepted, even honored, as though it made you appear more wanted in others' eyes.

But she and Jack weren't French. Despite their immense wealth, they were a typical American couple: in love, after many years of marriage's ups and downs. He hardly noticed the other women's eyes and instead turned his gaze toward her, smiled, and folded his paper. It was time to move forward.

Jack announced that dinner would be at eight. "It's an exclusive restaurant near the Louvre," he told her. "The waitlist is normally about a mile long if you can believe it."

"That's hardly a problem for the likes of Jack Potter."

Jack's grin widened. He hailed a taxi with a direct shot of his arm. A car immediately removed itself from the ever-charging line of vehicles and pulled up directly before them. "Dinner might be something of a surprise, though," he explained as they eased into the back seat.

"And why is that?"

Jack shrugged playfully. "I suppose you'll just have to see for yourself."

Janine placed her head against Jack's shoulder and watched the Parisian streets, captivated. A young boy held a bright red balloon and let it bob to and fro beneath the heavy raindrops; his mother wore this season's most expensive Prada spring jacket, which Janine had almost selected for herself; at the corner, a very tall woman held a pink umbrella over the top of a very short man who played the violin.

"It's all like a ridiculous postcard," she whispered.

"That's Paris, isn't it? Always some kind of cliché," Jack recited.

When they reached the restaurant, Chez Paul, Jack paid the driver just before he rushed around to open the door and assist Janine back out onto the damp streets. Jack placed his hand at the base of her back and led her toward the gorgeous entrance of the restaurant. Even from the door, Janine could see only four or five tables, making this one of the more exclusive, intimate dining locations in all of Paris. Candles flickered, casting a beautiful silhouette across the walls.

In the furthest corner, a familiar face peered out of the shadows. There, seated at a two-top, in this season's finest Dolce & Gabbana, wearing the sort of heels New York and Paris fashion-women dreamt about, with picture-perfect lipstick and model-like cheekbones, sat Janine's other favorite person in the world: Maxine Aubert.

Janine forgot herself. She forgot her place in the world, the nature of the restaurant, her status as Jack Potter's wife. At this moment, she was only a girl from Brooklyn, in full view of her best friend. She raced across the space, nearly bumping into a busboy en route to a neighboring table, and flung herself into Maxine's arms. Maxine slipped her chin across Janine's shoulder and giggled madly. If Janine closed her eyes and shifted her attention just-so, stripping them of their iconic styles and their sultry perfumes, she could almost imagine a younger version of herself, greeting Maxine at their local Brooklyn high school, back when everything had been much more sinister, and they'd only had one another.

"We got her, didn't we?" Maxine grinned toward Jack as he approached.

"Ooph. Am I crying?" Janine wiped the corners of her eyes delicately. "Safe to say I didn't see this coming. I had no idea you'd be in Paris this week!"

"Gregory flew me over a few days ago. It was spontaneous. Jack suggested we arrange this little birthday meeting and, well, darling, you know I wouldn't want to be anywhere else but with you on your birthday."

Janine sat across from Maxine as the waiter arrived to take their wine order. Jack remained standing as Maxine placed their order seamlessly, having never forgotten her childhood French language. Jack whistled, impressed.

"I would have ordered the same," he stated with a nod.

Maxine wagged her eyebrows. "Not bad for a girl from Brooklyn?"

"You should be honored. He rarely gives compliments," Janine said as her heart belled out of her chest. She then lifted her eyes toward Jack's. "Are you sure you don't want to stay for dinner?"

"No. You girls have your time together. I've been allowed an entire day with you and it was perfect. Besides, when you two get to talking, it's like I don't exist. It's not very good for my ego," Jack teased.

Janine and Maxine ordered a decadent five-course meal, including a to-die-for creme brûlée and a second bottle of wine. Their conversation eased seamlessly across many decades. They discussed the first day they met when Janine had stumbled on a stoop and cut her knee open and cried into Maxine's shoulder. At the time, Maxine hadn't known more than a few English words and had murmured little French songs into Janine's ear to try to calm her down.

"I'd heard French before and had always thought it sounded like the most magical thing," Janine commented. "I thought you were a magical princess from another world."

"And really, it was you who became the princess," Maxine pointed out. "When you met Jack? I thought for sure it was, well..."

"You thought he was using me. And you were probably very right in thinking that," Janine offered.

"But I was wrong. And I'm so glad to be wrong," Maxine told her, her eyes glowing with candlelight. "What you two have built together is beautiful."

Janine's thoughts stirred as she slipped back on her trench coat and grabbed the umbrella, which Jack had left for her. Jack had already pre-paid, something he always did, which left Janine and Maxine to step out into the soft drizzle and contemplate what came next. Like lost girls, they purchased a bottle of wine from a corner shop and then meandered through the streets to arrive at the River Seine, which surged through the central heart of Paris and crept around Notre Dame Cathedral. When they reached the glow of the cathedral, they removed their expensive high heels and perched at the brick side edge of the river with their feet dangling down below. The rain had stopped for now, and they forgot to care about mussing their coats. Maybe they would regret it later. Maybe not.

"Do you think you ever want to do it, Max?" Janine whispered before she took a small sip of wine, straight from the bottle— just as they'd done in long-ago days back in Brooklyn.

"Do what?"

"You know, the marriage thing. Have some children."

Maxine made a soft, hesitant noise in the base of her throat. Her eyes caught the soft glow of the enormous, old-world cathedral. How many other women across time and space had contemplated their lives from this very location? Maxine then accepted the bottle of wine and took her own sip before answering.

"I don't know. Sometimes, I think about it. About what it meant that day when I held Maggie in my arms as you slept in that hospital bed. I felt the enormity of what you'd done. You had brought a new life into this world. A new story. I wondered if I would ever be strong enough." She laughed quietly after that and then added, "And sometimes, I think I might be too selfish for it. I'm thirty-three, but I still feel I have so much life to live. So many men to meet."

Janine's smile widened. "As long as you keep me in the loop about all your adventures— all the men you know and love and all the people you meet."

"Maybe when the girls are older, you can come along with me," Maxine offered.

"Maybe," Janine added thoughtfully. "Although I can't help but be a sap where Jack is concerned. I picture us on a beach somewhere, holding hands and watching the sunset. Maybe by then, we'll be all shriveled up and tired. Maybe we won't have a single thing to say to one another. But I know my love for him will remain true. Forever."

Maxine shuddered and took another long sip of wine.

"What?" Janine asked with a laugh.

"You're right about one thing," Maxine teased. "You're a real sap."

Janine punched Maxine lightly on the shoulder as her heart

lifted. In the distance, a woman sang a melancholic French tune from an open window. Far above, clouds began to creep apart to reveal a large, pregnant moon.

"But actually, Jack knows the truth, doesn't he?" Janine countered. "That you're my real soulmate. That's why he brought us together tonight. That's why he's nowhere in sight."

Maxine laughed. "He knows nothing can bring us apart."

"We've been through so much already," Janine pointed out before gripping the wine bottle and taking it back. "I mean, look at us. We were diamonds in the rough and we'll always be Brooklyn girls for life."

Maxine lifted her pinky toward Janine and nodded toward it.

"You're suggesting we pinky swear?" Janine asked.

"It worked for us in the past. I don't know why it wouldn't work for us now."

"As thirty-three-year-olds?"

"Come on. We're not even middle-aged," Maxine offered. "In the prime of our lives. Let's pinky-swear to another seventy years together. Arm-in-arm at the nursing home, making fun of the other old ladies' fashion and doing each other's makeup and watching old *Friends* episodes and feeding each other mashed potatoes."

"Seventy years is quite a long time."

"We don't know that yet," Maxine replied. "We haven't lived it. As far as we know, it could feel like ten minutes."

"I sure hope not."

"Just pinky swear about it," Maxine insisted. "Be the greatest love of my life, as long as we both shall live."

"A little cliché to ask me this in front of Notre Dame Cathedral, isn't it?"

"Janine." Maxine's eyes widened playfully. "I swear if you don't pinky promise me..."

Janine snapped her free pinky into Maxine's and squeezed it hard. Maxine shook her hand violently as they both burst into laughter. Janine took a swig of wine, then passed it over to Maxine, who took her own celebratory sip. When their eyes met again, they swam in the promise of tomorrow— one built on the texture of old memories, the beauty of time spent. They'd never needed anyone else but one another. The future, as they saw it now, was bright.

# CHAPTER TWO

## PRESENT DAY

JANINE SQUATTED DOWN at the entry to the hall closet, hunting for Elsa's basket of party decorations, which she'd reportedly used for previous family functions at the house. Janine shifted through what seemed to be ten-year-old unused balloons, dusty streamers, and scrap paper, then clucked her tongue with regret. None of this would do for the party at hand. She then shifted back up onto her heels, rose to shut the door, then turned and immediately let out a blood-curdling scream.

A ghost stood between her and the kitchen.

But immediately, that ghost burst into a familiar, gut-belly laughter. Alyssa appeared beneath a white sheet and grinned madly at her mother.

"Happy Halloween!" she cried.

Janine's heartbeat wouldn't slow. She pressed her hand across her chest and exhaled deeply. "You know I'm easily freaked out!"

"It's almost too easy," Alyssa agreed. "Did you find anything?"

"Not really," Janine admitted as she exhaled deeper. "Maybe we should run to Edgartown. Grab some extra supplies."

In the living room, Mallory's one-year-old son, Zachery, let out a gut-wrenching shriek of his own. Janine's cries had apparently woken him.

"Now look what you've done," Maggie called before appearing in the hallway to give her younger sister an annoyed look. "Alyssa, look at yourself. How old are you?"

Alyssa stuck out her tongue playfully. "Oh, I get it. You're married and extremely mature now. Okay, noted."

Maggie rolled her eyes back into her head. "Mom, I can run to Edgartown if you want to get things done here. Any idea of what kind of decorations you might want?"

"I don't know. Anything that brings a birthday and Halloween party together," Janine replied. "Christine just wrote that she's headed here with the birthday cake. And Elsa?"

Elsa popped her head out from the kitchen. Her blonde highlights caught in the sterling light, beaming in from the bay windows that allowed for a beautiful view of the ocean out in the distance.

"Well, hello there. What do you need?"

"How are we on champagne? Wine? Beer?" Janine asked.

"I have Bruce out grabbing another few boxes of beer," Elsa reported. "But otherwise, I think we're all set."

Janine nodded as she stitched her eyebrows together. It was Carmella's forty-third birthday, and Janine, Elsa, and Nancy had conspired to make everything picture-perfect. Carmella had kept her distance from the family for ages, so much so that she hadn't had a birthday celebration in decades. When Janine had learned

Carmella's birthday was on Halloween itself, she suggested a full-blown celebration— one that would remind Carmella of how grateful they all were that she had decided to return herself, heart and all, to the Remington clan. Janine knew what it was like to feel like an outsider from a world you once belonged to. There was nothing like cake and a bit of bubbling champagne to bridge that divide.

"It's cold out there!" Janine called to Maggie as she headed for the door. "Grab your hat and scarf."

"I'll go with you!" Alyssa took two strides toward her own coat as Janine stepped back into the living area, where Mallory bobbed baby Zachery against her chest and blinked large, hooded eyes.

"When is Carmella supposed to arrive?" Mallory asked.

"Cody said he'd have her here around six-thirty," Janine replied. "It gives us about three hours to get everything done."

At that moment, Nancy charged down the staircase, having gone upstairs for a brief afternoon nap. Her recent health scares meant a good deal more time resting in bed, which she often complained about, as she was about as action-oriented as they came. "I hate the idea of missing out on anything because my body won't let me do it," she'd said once.

Now, Nancy smacked her palms together and demanded that Elsa and Janine put her to work. "I know for a fact there's clam chowder to stir up, biscuits to bake, and wine to drink," she declared, her smile electric.

Back in the kitchen, Elsa poured Janine and Nancy glasses of French Cabernet Sauvignon from Provence. Nancy yawned a final time before asking about the whereabouts of Maggie and Alyssa— her beautiful granddaughters.

"Where was it Rex ran off to this weekend?" Nancy asked as she arranged several onions onto a cutting board. "I swear, that husband of hers can't keep still."

"If it means she'll take more trips to the island, then I say we let Rex run off wherever he pleases," Elsa stated as she pressed her flour-tinged hands into the biscuit dough, kneading it with her full weight.

"We've got ourselves a pretty decent girls' club; I'd say," Nancy said as she pressed the knife through the first onion. "Martha's Vineyard Sisterhood or something like it."

"Men come and go, but all we need is each other," Janine offered with a laugh. "Oh! That reminds me. I think Henry will stop by. He's coming in from the city today."

Elsa and Nancy cast one another glances so slight that Janine only barely noticed. Neither had asked Janine about the nature of her and Henry's relationship, as things had been so chaotic since her big break-up with her ex-husband, Jack. Janine had sensed everyone thought of her like a ticking time bomb. *"Don't talk about the break-up. Don't talk about Jack. Don't talk about New York. And whatever you do, don't mention for a moment, Maxine Aubert."*

"Why was he in New York?" Elsa asked.

"He had a documentary in a small film festival," Janine replied.

Again, Elsa and Nancy exchanged glances. Janine placed her hand on her hip and glared at them.

"What's with all this over-the-counter mind-reading?" she demanded.

Elsa cleared her throat as Nancy responded.

"We just wonder, I guess, why you didn't go to his film festival? I mean, the two of you spend so much time together." Nancy spoke slowly, trying to articulate her words with gentleness so as not to put pressure on Janine.

Janine shrugged and turned back toward the ocean, which seemed overly volatile in the tumultuous October winds, which ripped over the waves without pause and despite the glowing sunshine above.

"I've seen the documentary many times now," Janine answered in a steady tone.

What she meant was: she couldn't return to the city. The idea of New York City, in general, made her shiver with fear. What if she ran into Jack? What if she saw Maxine? What if a single Brooklyn sight sent her into a spiral of memories so great that she had to return to bed to cry for the next week? On Martha's Vineyard, she was safe from her past; she'd carved out a new future with her mother and her stepsisters and her new friends, like Henry.

The door that led out to the main driveway opened, and with it came the sound of Bruce hollering hello. Elsa's face brightened like the sun. She grabbed a towel to swipe off her white-tinged hands, then hustled into his arms for a hug when he entered the kitchen with three large boxes of beer. Behind him came Cole, Elsa's twenty-six-year-old son, who apparently looked the spitting image of Elsa's deceased husband, Aiden.

"Look what I found out on the streets?" Bruce remarked with a funny laugh. "Recruited him for beer pick-up."

Elsa shrieked, then flung her arms around Cole, who wasn't often seen at the family house. He never did like crowds. He did, however, have his own small circle of friends that he hung with over at the sailing docks in Edgartown.

"I heard there's a party happening," Cole stated with a cheeky smile. "You trying to ruin Aunt Carmella's day?"

"Oh, stop it," Elsa returned as she gripped one of the boxes of beer and headed out toward the back porch, where they planned to store the beer in the chill while the party remained in the warm glow of the main house. "Did you at least bring a costume, like I asked you?"

Cole shrugged, reached into his back pocket, and then placed a Red Sox baseball hat on his head. "I'm a baseball player."

Elsa rolled her eyes. "That, my dear, is the lazier Halloween costume I've ever seen."

"Really, and what are you going as?" Cole demanded playfully.

"She's forced us into a couple costume if you can believe it," Bruce said under his breath, feigning annoyance.

"Let me guess," Cole said tentatively. "You're a Disney prince..."

"Oh, come on, I'm not that cruel," Elsa told him. "Bruce already had all the perfect hunting gear. And I'm going as a doe." She hustled over to a little tote bag, where she drew out some deer-ears and a little black nose, which she would glue onto herself later.

"Isn't that cute!" Nancy cried from her onion-slicing, where her eyes glowed from the intensity of the air around the knife.

"You don't have to cry about it, Nancy," Cole teased.

"And what about Carmella?" Bruce asked. "Are you forcing her to dress up, too?"

"We have a costume for her," Janine told him with a funny grin. "Cody helped us pick a couple's costume for him, Carmella, plus his daughter, Gretchen."

"Well, don't spill all the beans," Elsa hissed. "Cole gets

overwhelmed with cutesy stuff. He's apt to grab three beers for himself and run out the door."

"Don't tempt me, Mom."

There was a knock at the door. Janine hustled back into the living room and then to the foyer to open it. On the other side, she found Christine Sheridan, who had agreed to bake a "spooky" Halloween-Birthday cake for Carmella. The cake was wrapped up, as was Christine, in a beautiful burgundy Peabody coat with a thickly layered scarf wrapped around her neck. Even her beautiful coat failed to hide her pregnant belly.

"Mind if I come in for a sec?" she asked with shivering lips.

Once inside, Christine placed the cake tenderly on the counter and rubbed her palms together as Nancy, Janine, and Elsa gathered around to unwrap and ogle Christine's artistic creation. As usual, Christine had outdone herself. She had crafted little ghouls and ghosts out of fondant; they seemed to float out of a cave, which was surrounded with beautiful, scary pine trees, which rolled down either side of the cake, toward a much larger cave, with two large eyes peering out of the darkness. In large, beautiful, curled letters, Christine had written, *"HAPPY BIRTHDAY, CARMELLA."*

"It's a salted caramel cake," Christine explained. "But I dyed all the fondant to make it, you know, Halloween-relevant."

Nancy passed Christine a mug of tea, which she accepted gratefully.

"You must have so much on your plate," Nancy offered then. "You've got Baby Max at your place, along with another little one on the way..."

Christine grimaced. "Max is a handful. He has all the character of his mother, Audrey, along with these huge, gut-busting lungs that allow him to screech over the waters of the Vineyard Sound, but still, Zach and I love him to pieces."

Janine laughed good-naturedly. "How's his momma doing at school?"

"She misses her baby so much." Christine's eyes sparkled with sorrow. "She comes back from Penn State as often as she can and talks a lot about doing online classes so she can come back for good. I think she thought it would be a whole lot easier than it is."

"You couldn't have taken me away from my babies when they were that little," Elsa agreed as she lifted a hand to pat Cole's cheek playfully, lovingly.

"I guess I'll know what that's like very soon..." Christine said brightly as she splayed a hand over her stomach. "The Sheridan family just keeps getting bigger and bigger. But with Maggie married, now, you must have some ideas of what's next for you, Janine?"

Janine's eyes widened slightly at the thought. She only half remembered when she and Jack had laughed about the concept of being grandparents. "I'll love you when you're old and grey and too fat for your pants," she had told him once in a sing-song voice as he'd grimaced. Now, at forty-three and mostly single, the idea of being a grandmother was far different than it had been before.

Christine left just as Maggie and Alyssa arrived with a treasure trove of celebratory decor. Elsa instructed Mallory, Cole, Maggie, and Alyssa what to do next to prepare for the party ahead. Very soon, Cody would return to the house, with Carmella and Gretchen in tow. Everything had to be ready. Elsa's perfectionism had fully taken over, and everyone else had to get in line.

# CHAPTER THREE

CODY'S CAR was a bright white dot at the far end of the driveway. Nancy shrieked, "Everyone! Places! They're here!" And in a moment, they scrambled to all corners of the living room, hallway, kitchen, and dining area, all of them in costumes that ranged from all-out to barely-there (Cole in his baseball hat, for example, or baby Zachery, who had wept when Mallory had put on his tiger costume, which had led to Mallory deciding he would just go as himself). Janine had donned an Audrey Hepburn Breakfast at Tiffany's get-up, complete with a pearl necklace and long white gloves. When she had shown it off for Henry the night before his departure for New York, he'd shivered and glanced down at the floor before saying, "Yeah, it looks great." It had felt like a layered response. Janine hadn't known what to do with it.

From Janine's hiding place on one side of the window, tucked behind the curtain, she had a full view of Cody and Carmella as they hovered outside the back door of his car to get Gretchen out of her car seat. It had been a privilege to watch Carmella acknowledge her feelings for her best friend, Cody, who had always loved her in return, despite his brief foray of marriage with another woman, which had resulted in Gretchen. Carmella had confessed only once to Janine that she'd never imagined love would happen for her. Janine had marveled at the intimacy of the confession, but in the wake of it, she had retreated to her room and wept.

After all, Janine had been in love once upon a time. It had been a wonderful thrill, the rush of a lifetime. And then, on one fateful night, her lovely dreams of friendship and romance had crumbled before her, proving themselves to be nothing but a farce.

Carmella lifted toddler Gretchen to her hip, handling her like a well-seasoned mother rather than Cody's girlfriend. Her smile was infectious as she chatted with Cody, even as the chilly wind gusted around them, yanking at their scarves and threatening to tear their hats from their heads. Cody had told Elsa his plan: to tell Carmella that he'd arranged for a restaurant reservation and that Elsa had agreed to babysit Gretchen for the night. Carmella, head in the clouds with love for her new beau, had believed the lie.

The door creaked open just the slightest bit, not enough to allow Carmella to enter.

"You good?" Cody asked. "She's getting so big."

"Oh, we're fine, aren't we, Gretch?" Carmella's voice seemed to belong to someone far different than the woman Janine had been introduced to back in June. "It looks dark in there. Are you sure Elsa's home?"

Janine caught sight of Cody's crooked grin through the crack of the door. With a vibrant rush, he pushed open the door fully, just as all family members burst out from their hiding places, snapped on the lights, then called out, "Happy Birthday, Carmella!"

Carmella stepped through the door, her eyes enormous with surprise. Maggie and Alyssa had bought everyone little whistles and party buzzers, which created the world's most annoying chorus, echoing from all sides. Carmella's eyes filled with tears.

"You've got to be kidding me!" she cried through the commotion.

Gretchen grew distracted and tossed herself around Carmella's torso until Carmella placed her delicately on the floor, only for her to hustle up to Elsa, dressed up as a deer, who scooped her up just as quickly. She then walked directly to her sister and flung her free arm around her as Carmella descended into tears.

"This is too much!" Carmella cried.

"You know us Remington girls will do anything for a party," Elsa told her.

Carmella pulled away from the embrace to feign an angry growl at Cody for being a partner in crime. "You were in on it!"

Cody lifted his palms skyward and replied, "I'm guilty, but don't shoot. You know I'll do anything for cake."

Carmella lifted up on her tip-toes to plant a kiss on Cody's lips. She then returned her eyes to Elsa before catching sight of Bruce, dressed head-to-toe in camouflage. "Ah-hah. Couple costume! Who else do we have around here? Cole, I see you went all-out, as usual."

"Guilty as charged," Cole nodded, adjusting his simple baseball hat.

"And Janine! Wow, Audrey Hepburn. Get over here," Carmella insisted, beckoning for Janine, who fell into a hug. She whispered sweet greetings into Carmella's ear as her heart surged.

She had been allowed to watch this woman rise from the ashes. That was certainly something to celebrate— not just another year around the sun.

Maggie and Alyssa were dressed as teenage Mary Kate and Ashley Olsen, who they'd been borderline obsessed with as youngsters. A few times since those early days, they had been photographed partying with the Olsen twins, as Alyssa and Maggie still belonged to that upper-echelon high-society Manhattan world, the one Janine felt excommunicated from. When Janine had asked how the Olsen twins might feel about Alyssa and Maggie dressing up as them for Halloween, Alyssa had said, "Oh my gosh, Mom, they're iconic. They never get on social media, and they barely deign to know our names. We'll be okay." "Yeah, Mom, they barely know the name of their only other sister," Maggie had highlighted.

Nancy had Cody, Carmella, and Gretchen's costumes set up off to the side: Peter Pan, Wendy, and Tinker Bell. They slipped into one of the downstairs guest rooms to change, then re-emerged to many flashes of multiple phone cameras, behind which their users "oohed" and "ahhed."

"Jeez, the paparazzi in this place is hideous," Carmella joked.

Nancy corralled everyone into the kitchen, where they collected large bowls of clam chowder and biscuits and then headed out toward the beach, where Bruce had built a large bonfire. Janine hovered toward the back of the line, waiting her turn and listening to the chaos of her newfound family's conversation. The click of the front door behind her forced her back around to find Henry— her bright light in the darkness, one of her newest yet truest friends. She had told him just once that she couldn't have gotten through summer without him— his laughter, his artistry, his ability to turn anything on its head and show her a different perspective, and of course, his affinity for short but beautiful sailing expeditions.

"There she is. My breakfast at Tiffany," he said brightly as he stepped toward her, his camera strap tight over his chest.

Janine felt that jump in her gut again, this ever-simmering desire to kiss him. They'd only kissed a handful of times, each of which she had eventually called a "mistake." She wasn't ready; she'd been through too much. She wouldn't be surprised if Henry decided to move on from her very soon. He was handsome; he was almost famous; he would one day be a world-renowned documentarian, with a beautiful artist or actress on his arm at various film festivals around the globe. She would still be there, on Martha's Vineyard, where he assuredly didn't belong.

"You made it!" she said instead as if her mind didn't stir in a million other directions.

"Of course. I said I would, didn't I?"

They hugged, and it felt anticlimactic as if their bodies wanted so much more. Janine dropped her eyes to the ground and then inhaled deeply to regroup.

"Where's your costume?" she teased.

"I'm the filmmaker," Henry returned as he tapped his camera bag. "And the man behind the camera never needs a costume."

She cocked an eyebrow. "Hmm. Sounds like an easy out. Have you been talking with my nephew?"

Nancy popped her head out of the kitchen and beckoned the two of them in to grab their bowls of chowder and head out to the bonfire. "I think it's going to be a beautiful sunset," she noted. "I don't think we should miss it."

The bonfire kicked up a hissy fit, flickering wildly toward the vibrant oranges, pinks, and yellows of the brewing sunset. Janine hovered near Henry, Alyssa, and Maggie, as Henry told them about the recent film festival in the city. The three of them spoke about New York— Janine's city, as though it was the only place in the world. Janine's heart felt squeezed with jealousy.

"Not a huge fan of this year's styles," Alyssa said absent-mindedly. "What did you wear?"

"You know I'm a documentarian, right?" Henry joked. "If we wear more than a pair of jeans and a white t-shirt, we should be given a medal."

To Maggie and Alyssa, film festivals were about glamor, about seeing and being seen. They'd, of course, gotten this from their father's world— a world Janine had been lucky to call her own for so long. Henry wasn't like this in the slightest, something Janine adored about him.

"You really shouldn't have, Elsa." This was Carmella, on the far side of the flickering flame, as she opened Elsa's gift. Within the small box was a simple, delicate diamond necklace, which caught the light beautifully. Carmella's smile faltered just the slightest bit. Janine had a hunch Carmella thought the gift was "too much," especially given that Carmella would never have as much money as her sister. Elsa probably would never comprehend the gap between the two of them, not the way Janine could, being an outsider and also a woman who had lived on both extreme sides of the poverty line.

Money was a complex thing. She'd done her darnedest to raise her daughters without surly arrogance, the likes of which Jack Potter had been raised with throughout his youth.

An hour or so later, they gathered in the kitchen to sing "Happy

Birthday" and cut the cake. Carmella lifted Gretchen up just after the song to allow her to slide her finger along the goopy edge of the frosting, which Christine had used to form the little bushes in the forest. Gretchen slopped the frosting across her tongue and shrieked with happiness.

"Oh, to be a kid eating frosting on Halloween. Does it get any better than that?" Carmella asked before she planted a kiss on Gretchen's cheek.

Nancy, Janine, and Elsa became an immediate assembly line: a slice of cake followed by one or two dollops of Neapolitan ice cream, which they'd decided was especially festive. Everyone also got a few little Halloween gummies on their plate, including a bat, a tiny pumpkin, and a ghost, for good measure.

"You three really went all out for me," Carmella remarked from the doorway between the kitchen and the dining room, her hand balancing a glass of red wine. She looked half-tipsy, and her cheeks glowed slightly, as though she was just a young girl, happy and exhausted after her birthday.

"You deserve it, honey," Nancy beamed.

"I don't know about that. I do feel like the luckiest woman in the world," Carmella returned, then took another bite of her cake.

Janine stepped back onto the porch with her own slab of cake and morsel of ice cream. Henry stood out there in the gathering darkness. The orange light caught against the upper part of his cheeks and echoed over the curve of his eyes. Janine was captivated by him. She stepped over and sidled up against him as her nose filled with his musk. Years before, she had cowered from the sight of Jack, even after a decade of marriage. He'd intoxicated her in a far different way; perhaps she'd been frightened of him or simply frightened of the power he had over her. Henry had a different power, a quiet one.

From high up on the porch, the two of them watched the party continue on. Bruce placed another log onto the fire, then another, which the fire ate up hungrily. Stan Ellis, who had been staying at the Lodge since the hurricane sent a crater through his house, arrived, then grabbed a bowl of clam chowder and soon fell into conversation with Nancy on two garden chairs near the ocean line. Maggie and Alyssa were feeling loose and free and in the midst of a handstand competition. They'd recruited Gretchen, who contributed to the contest with a half-somersault. This left all three girls in stitches.

"You have such a wonderful family," Henry breathed.

Janine turned to steal a glance at him, then smiled. "I can't believe it, either. It's been such a whirlwind."

Again, silence. Janine began to regret standing near Henry like this. It felt like staring at the beast directly in the eyes, without knowing if that beast planned to eat you.

Henry's lips parted. Janine sensed he wanted to say something important, something that would change everything. She wanted to stay in the in-between forever, without making any kind of choice. How could she possibly move on from all her heartbreak? How could she make herself vulnerable to get her heart broken all over again?

A moment passed. Janine closed her eyes as one of Henry's hands closed over hers in the dark. When Jack had first fallen for her, she'd felt his desire for her like a powerful tide, pulling her under. She could resist Henry if she wanted to, whereas she hadn't been able to resist Jack. He wouldn't have allowed it.

"Henry, I..."

But before she could finish her thought, there was a horrible scream in the distance. Janine's eyes popped open. Henry removed his hand from hers as she bolted from the porch, knowing that scream to be Alyssa's and only Alyssa's. This wasn't a playful scream; this had nothing to do with her silly handstands in the sand.

Janine's daughters were both on all fours on the sand. Nancy hovered over them, demanding to know what was wrong. Alyssa's phone was positioned across her palm as Maggie wailed.

"No. No, no, no..." Alyssa fretted the same syllable over and over again. "No."

Janine dropped to her knees and found Maggie's eyes. Maggie was now quiet, but her shoulder shook back and forth with shock. Janine splayed her hand over Maggie's knee and gripped Alyssa's wrist, the one that secured her phone screen. Slowly, Janine forced herself to read the upside-down font displayed on the screen of Alyssa's phone.

In dark letters, she read words that seemed impossible.

They seemed outside of time, taken from a book of someone else's life.

**JACK POTTER, MANHATTAN BILLIONAIRE, FOUND DEAD**

# CHAPTER FOUR

## MAXINE AUBERT

"YOU'RE JEALOUS OF HER. Aren't you?" These words whispered to Maxine just after Janine and Jack had said their vows at their iconic, five-hundred-person wedding in Manhattan twenty years before, now sizzled through her memory.

The speaker had been Jack Potter's cousin, Rhonda, a plump and big-toothed young woman with a bodice that had squashed her breasts and spilled the top half of them over, like the upper part of a cupcake.

"Excuse me?" Maxine had said at the time, adjusting her giant bouquet, an overkill (in her opinion) of lilies and baby's breath, styled by the at-the-time top-tier florist in all of Manhattan.

Rhonda had had a wad of gum between her teeth. Her eyes had glittered with malice. "You girls from Brooklyn— you all want a piece of our Manhattan world."

At this, Maxine had leaned toward her and whispered, "I know your type, Rhonda. You wouldn't share a piece of anything if your life depended on it." She'd then yanked herself around, drummed up a picture-perfect smile, and prepared herself for a horrific, two-hour journey through photography hell. One of those photos had graced the cover of the Sunday *New York Times*. At the time, Maxine's father had snipped the photo out of the newspaper and hung it on his fridge in Brooklyn, in his first-ever act of allegiance toward anything Maxine had involved herself in.

Maxine was now forty-three years old and much richer than she'd ever imagined herself to be, even in her wildest dreams. She was also dreadfully alone. Her father was dead, as was the very rich man who'd married her in her mid-thirties and eventually left her an enormous sum of money. When Maxine had said her vows, aligning her life with the much-older Jim, she'd thought again of Jack's cousin Rhonda. Had she been jealous all those years ago? Had she only social-climbed her way alongside Janine as a way to prove herself? Had she ever fallen for Jim at all?

Maxine hadn't gotten dressed since she'd found him.

She now sat in an old Yankees t-shirt that fluttered to her knees, taken years ago from an ex-lover. The mirror told her a story of a woman who very suddenly looked her age, after many years of being told that she looked much younger. Her cheekbones were overly sharp due to a sudden weight loss. Once on the streets of Paris, a young man had demanded she come to his studio to be photographed in the nude. Nobody would demand such a thing, not now. Beauty had always been a fleeting thing for other women; time hadn't been meant to come to her.

Here it was.

And Jack was dead.

When she'd found him on the floor of the bedroom he'd once

shared with Janine, Maxine had felt next-to-nothing. They'd had plans to meet for dinner that evening, a brand-new Thai place on the Upper West Side, which was said to be the next big thing.

Perhaps the fact that she had felt nearly nothing at all destroyed her the most. After all, she'd given up everything for him. She'd destroyed the greatest love she had ever known. Now, she had money— buckets of it, and not a whole lot else. "We can burn money, baby, and we'd still have more," was something Jim had said to her on a particularly crazy trip to Shanghai. The notion had troubled her; her stomach had strained with sickness. Still, she'd laughed and carried on with him, as though she'd never been that struggling little girl from Brooklyn.

"9-1-1-, what is your emergency?'

*Hello. A man who has been cruel to me for the past six months has died on his bedroom floor.* This was her immediate thought.

But what was it she'd really said? Something that left out all personal details. She'd made sure the ambulance arrived as soon as possible and made sure to say all the correct things. When he'd gone, she'd left Janine's apartment (a place she could only think of as Janine's apartment) and wandered back to her own, alone. It was only when she arrived to the doorman that she realized she'd walked through the rain without a coat or umbrella, like a woman lost in thought.

Jack had died on Halloween. A massive heart attack had taken him.

A simple death for an overly complex, overly cruel man. A man who'd spent the last months of his life belittling Maxine, making a once-proud woman feel about four inches tall.

*"How can you deal with yourself?"* This had been a question

from another high-society lady a few months before, when she'd attended a gala, her arm wrapped delicately over Jack's. At events like that, she'd always felt like Jack's little piece of jewelry; something delegated to make sure he looked a certain way.

Maxine hadn't answered this question. They'd been stationed at the bathroom mirrors, fixing their hair and lipstick across middle-aged faces. Being a socialite meant always looking your best at all times.

"*I mean, your best friend,*" *the woman had clucked.* "*Men are cruel enough to us. Why would you help them?*"

The bell rang. Maxine blinked down at her Yankees t-shirt and stumbled off the edge of the bed. She remained there, taking stock of the way she held her weight over her feet, waiting. Who was at the door? Had someone said they were coming to visit? Who could that have been? She didn't know anyone. She had nobody.

Again, the bell rang. It caused an immediate ringing sensation between Maxine's ears, so much so that she clenched her eyes closed. Admittedly, she had spent the previous few days in the midst of some kind of bender, alternating between wine and whiskey. She was reminded of Nancy Grimson back in the old Brooklyn days when she had been wild with non-stop boozing. At Maggie's wedding, Nancy's skin had glowed with health and vitality; her eyes had been bright lights of energy and intelligence. Maxine had seen none of that other version of Nancy— not till now when she looked in the mirror.

"All right. All right." Maxine hobbled toward the front door of her high-rise apartment suite, with its exhaustive view of Central Park down below. A view of Central Park was meant to be one of the best views in the universe— the kind of thing you swapped your soul for. Maxine no longer looked out the window. She felt she'd seen it enough.

Maxine ripped open the door to discover three intrusive paparazzi members wielding cameras. The flashes felt insulting and pointed; she immediately lost her sense of vision and cried out, both in French and English.

"Get the hell out of here! Arrête! Out!" She thrust her body forward so that her fingers blasted against the lenses. With all her might, she pushed the men back, then swung her toe back to clip the door closed. As she finalized the distance between them, the cameramen took more shots of her, several of them featuring her haggard expression, her stick legs as they stuck out beneath the t-shirt, and her unwashed hair. Jack had once described her as the most beautiful woman he'd ever seen, but now Jack was dead.

He was dead. She had to remind herself of this as she returned to her bedroom, where she slammed the door closed to prove some kind of point.

Back at her armoire, she studied her fingers, which were chipped, as she'd missed her manicure appointment from two days before. Jack's funeral was set to begin in three hours. Could she make it? What on earth could she possibly wear?

It wasn't that she didn't have an iconic collection of fantastic French designer clothing. It was simply that she'd forgotten how to exist as a person in society.

She opened her jewelry box as a first step. Pearls. Pearls would almost certainly do. She eased them across the wood of the armoire and studied their milky interior. She no longer appreciated fine things the way she had when she'd first arrived at them. She and Janine had previously rifled through old antique collections and flea markets to find near-perfect, high-quality designer outfits. This was how Janine had arrived upon her Chanel dress, which she had worn to her first date with Jack Potter, that sultry-hot billionaire who had asked her out after she'd waitressed for him.

"I'll just go for the story," Janine had told Maxine at the time.

How had everything become so messy? Did it have to do with money? Power? Sex? Jealousy?

A combination of all of them, Maxine supposed.

Something caught Maxine's eye within the jewelry box. She peered within as she eased her fingers along the unique little pieces she'd collected from her rendezvous around the world. Yet there, stationed at the very base of the box, was something she hadn't seen in years.

One-half of a friendship necklace, purchased from the mall when she and Janine had been no more than thirteen years old.

Maxine immediately burst into tears at the sight of it. She lifted the necklace into the air— the cheap metal chain with its hanging one-half of a heart, which had ST on top and ENDS beneath it. For whatever reason, the ridiculousness of this mall-purchased necklace alongside her beautiful, expensive garb made her cry even more as it brought up an onslaught of gut-wrenching memories. She and Janine were representative of that necklace— lost in a world neither of them should have ever been privy to.

Well, she was lost in it. Janine had left and found a new path forward. She'd been incredibly kind and loyal and loving— and the world had paid her back handsomely. The world had paid Maxine for what she'd done, too. The outcome just wasn't as cozy as she'd thought it would be. Karma, she supposed.

Maxine latched the shoddy necklace around her neck. It hung

over the old Yankees' slogan foolishly. She was a forty-three old woman wearing kids' clothing in a high-rise apartment with a full view of the Park. In three hours, she was meant to go to her lover's funeral. During one of her and Jack's last conversations before his death, he'd told her, point-blank, that he would never marry her. "I'll never make that mistake again," he'd stated.

Due to some sort of idiocy within her, Maxine had wanted to protest, to tell him that actually, he'd had many beautiful years with Janine. She remembered them well, watching as the two of them became parents, fell deeper in love, took trips to Paris, to Tokyo, to Buenos Aires and beyond. But arguing in favor of Janine hadn't been in her best interest since she'd betrayed her.

What had she felt the first time Jack had kissed her? A rush of impossible feeling— for she'd finally captured that ever-forbidden thing, the thing she'd always reached for. She had always wanted what Janine had. Rhonda had been correct. Wretched Rhonda.

Maxine eyed herself in the mirror yet again as she gripped the stem of her wine glass, something to sip as she prepared herself for the hours ahead. She was the wretched one. She was the stupid one. And soon, she would face the real music of what she'd done— with many decades of loneliness and an ever-constant question.

Had it really been worth it?

# CHAPTER FIVE

JANINE DIDN'T HAVE to be told that Maxine was the one who found Jack. It seemed obvious, like saying the sky was blue or the ocean deep. Her best friend in the world had walked in to find the dead body of the man they'd both loved— and now, there was nothing left to do but heal and move on.

Janine had never spent an autumn away from the city. It was her favorite season, an era of chunky sweaters and gorgeous knee-high boots and fluttering scares; it was the season of *When Harry Met Sally* and long walks through Central Park and hot toddies at cocktail bars. The city leaned in a bit, whispered to you ahead of the dark chaos of the winter.

From high on the forty-third floor of the high-rise apartment building Janine had once lived in with Jack and her daughters, Janine found herself reckoning with a life she'd once thought would be hers forever. Many of her clothes remained in the very same walk-in closet, which she'd spent the better part of the previous

March organizing. The clothes looked totally foreign to her: cocktail dresses and blazers and beautiful Oscar de la Rente gowns from various functions over the years. If she wasn't mistaken, a particularly heinous dark green number from an up-and-coming French designer had been her choice for Henry's documentary premiere, which Jack had monetarily supported. That had been before she'd properly met Henry— before so much. She wouldn't have been caught dead in that outfit now.

"Mom?" Maggie's voice rang out from the foyer as the door creaked open. "Are you here?"

Janine inspected herself a final time in the mirror. She had chosen to wear an understated black dress, along with soft makeup and wavy hair that had been easy to do. Her personality for this event was a much more difficult thing to plan for. How did one "perform" for the funeral of a man who'd jumped ship for the hot best friend? What was one meant to say, "Sorry for your loss?" She hadn't lost him. She even knew exactly where he was just then; she'd spent the morning at the funeral home, making sure everything was in order. She was still his estranged wife, after all.

And now, it was up to her to ensure things went smoothly, if only for Maggie and Alyssa's sakes.

Maggie had gone for the understated look while Alyssa's dress plunged dangerously low. Although perhaps she would have said something in another year, just now, Janine was in no mood to point this out. At twenty-two, Alyssa could deal with her grief however she pleased, and Janine was quite done with any attempt to "please" the high-society people in Jack's world.

With their eyes tinged red with confusion and shock, Maggie and Alyssa tipped their heads onto Janine's shoulder. Alyssa let out a single sob while Maggie remained silent. It was terribly quiet in the old living room, a space they'd once shared as a family. In another dimension, Jack sat just there, in his favorite yellow chair, with the paper spread out across his lap as he scanned the headlines.

Janine wanted to say something, something that mattered. But each thought that came up— a suggestion that their father had loved them very much, that the world had been a better place with him in it, seemed false, especially after all he'd put them through the previous year. Sometimes, death was meaningless.

The doorman hailed a cab for them and told them how sorry he was for their loss. Alyssa, Maggie, and Janine hummed their response as the doorman pressed the door closed. Once inside, Alyssa told the driver, "Cathedral of the St. John the Divine," which was one of the largest cathedrals in the world and certainly the most beautiful in all of New York City— only the best for the likes of the Potter family. Janine's stomach threatened to vomit its contents, but she swallowed a gulp of water from a bottle and focused on the sights and sounds of her favorite version of New York, which lurked just outside the window.

During her worst moments, she was oddly grateful that Jack Potter wouldn't be around any longer to belittle Maggie and Alyssa or use his money to buy their love for him.

She knew these thoughts were poisonous, but there they were, lurking in the back of her mind.

"I can't believe you agreed to speak," Alyssa mumbled into Maggie's ear.

Maggie shrugged and folded up her scribed letter, which she planned to read during the service.

"I mean, come on, Maggie," Alyssa continued as she dug her elbow into Maggie's side.

"Lay off." Maggie's nostrils flared out. "I'm not sure if you missed the memo, but we only get one dad our entire lives. This is his funeral. I'm going to say a few words. Sue me."

The girls were silent for the rest of the drive. When they arrived at the Cathedral, Maggie's husband, Rex, awaited in a suit. He leaned down and opened the door, bringing the three Potter girls onto the sidewalk. When Janine paid the driver, he, too, told her how sorry he was. She would have paid for him to take that back, but he sped off before she could verbalize it. Her shoes were unsteady at the edge of the sidewalk. Alyssa gripped her elbow and tugged her back so that she joined the first edging of the crowd as it eased into the Cathedral. All eyes glued themselves to her and her daughters. Maggie allowed herself the slightest of smiles in greeting while Alyssa scowled at them, her face heavy with vitriol.

They'd met the priest the previous afternoon after the viewing. He was a very short elderly man with liver-spotted hands and watery eyes. Apparently, he'd performed the funerals for both of Jack's parents; beyond that, apparently, Janine had spoken with him prior to both services. It was as though that era of her life had been blanked out of her mind.

He greeted them personally in the front row of the Cathedral. His hand was chapped from the frigid New York winds. He spoke gently to Maggie about her portion of the service, explaining when he would need her at the pulpit while Alyssa tore at the edges of her leaflet. On the front page, their father's face peered back, unsmiling. Janine had been the one to select the photo; nobody else had been around to perform the task.

Perhaps the worst part of all of this was her broken heart. What Jack had done to her at Maggie's engagement party (and the months before, without her knowing) had been like a sledgehammer to the chest.

"Oh god. Not her," Janine muttered under her breath as a woman named Margot approached from the back, bringing with her a wave of ridiculous perfume.

Margot swept into the row behind the three of them and placed her hand on Janine's shoulder. Janine couldn't remember them ever speaking about anything more than a few recipes or the way they styled their hair. Did that mean "closeness"? Did that mean "speak with tenderness at husband's funeral"?

"Oh, I am just so sorry for your loss," Margot murmured from behind.

"Thank you," Maggie and Alyssa replied in a polite tone.

Margot waited for Janine to say something. Janine could have waited the rest of her life to speak. She thought about what it would mean to do that to poor Margot: stare at her, making eye contact, until the dawn of time. Margot might melt to the floor as a result, but before Janine could ruin Margot's afternoon, Nancy appeared in the aisle just behind her, followed shortly behind by Carmella and Elsa. Janine's heart jumped into her throat. She retreated from Margot's horrific, pitying eyes and fell into a group hug with her stepsisters and her mother, who knew exactly what to say— which in this instance, was nothing at all.

Maggie, Alyssa, Janine, Nancy, Elsa, and Carmella sat in a line together, the Martha's Vineyard's extended Remington-Grimson-Potter family, and waited for the service to begin. Rex, Maggie's husband, sat directly behind them as though he couldn't penetrate the powerful female force they'd created.

Nancy splayed a hand over Janine's, exhaled softly, and then whispered, "It's a whirlwind to be in the city again, isn't it?"

Janine nodded somberly. "Is everything okay at the Lodge?"

"You don't have to worry about the Lodge right now," Nancy murmured. "We took care of everything. Carmella and Elsa plan to drive back after the service."

The last thing Janine wanted was for Jack Potter to affect the thing she currently loved the most: the Katama Lodge and Wellness Spa.

"But I'll be around for the wake," Nancy continued. "Completely prepared to spend all of it in the kitchen, putting together cheese and cracker platters."

Janine wiped away a tear with the sleeve of her overly expensive dress, something she would never have done had Jack been around. "That's the thing about a Potter party, Mom. I hired someone to put together the cheese platters so that we can be tortured with endless conversations with people who want to impress us for no reason at all."

Nancy grimaced but soon corrected her face. "If you want me to speak to a pretentious wife of so-and-so about her recent life-altering meditation retreat in the Balkans or facial-peeling-treatment, I'm your girl."

"You're a life-saver," Janine breathed.

Toward the middle of the Cathedral rows, a familiar man appeared. Janine's eyes flickered toward her mother as Nancy caught sight of him: Maddox, a man she'd had a brief affair with over the course of Maggie's wedding and the weeks after when she had learned that her health scares were nothing to worry about. He stopped short in the center of the aisle, his hands in his pockets and his eyes smoldering. Nancy and Maddox seemed to regard one another as though nobody else in the Cathedral existed. You could have pierced the tension with a knife. Maddox then bowed his head and slipped into a row as Nancy righted herself.

Janine wondered what was up with that, if Nancy had given up on her millionaire lover from the city or decided to call it "just a fling." Nancy creased the edges of her own pamphlet, matching Alyssa's nervous energy. At this moment, the priest decided to take to the pulpit to begin the ceremony.

Everything felt like a cartoon version of someone else's life. The priest began with a number of pleasantries, then described the man in the shiny bronze coffin before them (closed, as per Jack's request in his will) as a family man, a successful businessman, and a wonderful, confident, and dedicated member of his community. Hearing this, Janine wanted to stand up and demand why a man who'd been gifted a trust fund just for being his lineage was termed "successful." Perhaps a funeral wasn't the time to workshop a man's life.

After a Biblical reading, it was Maggie's turn to take over the pulpit. Her steps were wayward; her heels clacked sporadically against the hardwood as she adjusted herself. Her first words into the microphone were hazy. Janine knew she would beat herself up for it later.

"Good afternoon," Maggie began. "My name is Maggie Potter, and I am the first child of Jack Potter— a man I knew and loved my whole life long."

Janine's stomach stirred. Back in the far-away olden days,

45

Maggie had very much loved her father. The girls both had. They'd scampered onto his lap after his arrival back home, demanding books to be read and stories to be told and games to be played.

There was a sound toward the back of the Cathedral: the creak of a door, then a shuffling, as though someone stumbled on their hands and knees through the doorway. Maggie's eyes fluttered up from her written page as she balked for a split-second. Her eyes found Janine's, giving her some kind of alert.

Janine drew her eyes back toward the far end of the Cathedral. There, standing in a slim, low-cut black dress, which revealed long, slender, gorgeous legs, was Janine's best friend, Maxine. Over the black dress, she'd opted for a fur coat, one she'd purchased in Milan with Janine on a spontaneous trip they'd taken in their mid-thirties. Beyond her overly expensive garb, she looked absolutely terrible. Black lines dripped from her eyes down her cheeks, and her hair was a chaotic lion's mane, the stuff of avant-garde magazines.

The moment Maxine's eyes found Janine's, she stumbled off to the side and gripped the edge of a pew to stabilize herself. Her knees clacked together dangerously. At the pulpit, Maggie stumbled over her words. It seemed unlikely she could weave her way back to her planned speech, not with this woman hovering in the back making a mess of things (yet again).

"Go," Nancy whispered suddenly. "You're the only one who can."

Janine inhaled sharply and drew herself to her feet. Although she resented this fact, she knew her mother was right. She walked around the side of the pew as Maggie eased herself back into her speech.

"He was a powerful force, my dad, the kind of man who always got what he wanted from life. He had a way with words— as though he'd invented the English language himself. He used to quiz me about the meaning of difficult words when I was a kid. I remember some of them; agelast, a person who never laughs or accismus, which is a form of irony where you pretend you're indifferent toward something you want a lot. Oh, and zenith was one I liked a lot. The highest point of something," Maggie continued.

Janine neared the far end of the Cathedral. Maxine had collapsed fully in a pew and stretched out her thin body across the seat as though it served as a therapist's chair.

In the pulpit, Maggie continued to speak. "I remember being at the top of the Eiffel Tower with him when Dad took my sister and I on a trip in our teenage years. He asked where we were. Alyssa said paradise. I said the 'zenith,' remembering the old word lessons from my childhood. That night, he let me drink my first glass of wine, a Domaine Leroy Musigny Grand Cru. He told me I could be whatever I wanted to be in this life, that I had the bravery and the knowledge to make it happen. I don't know if he was right. But I'll never forget that glass of wine or the intensity of his eyes..."

Janine hovered over Maxine's lithe body. Maxine's eyes were slightly open but seemed unseeing. A wave of alcohol came off her breath. It seemed probable that she'd lost fifteen pounds since Janine had last seen her at Maggie's wedding.

Weddings and funerals. It was the old adage, where you spotted people as you got older. Here was her "ride or die" best friend; here was the woman she would have given her life to only a year before.

Suddenly, Maxine's eyes popped open. She found Janine before her, gasped, and placed her heels onto the ground again. In a moment, with more energy than Janine had thought possible,

Maxine propelled herself into the aisle and back out into the foyer. She was reminded of a gazelle, sweeping across the African landscape and away from predators.

Several people toward the back of the Cathedral turned their heads to watch the chase. Maggie stumbled yet again. Janine didn't dare look up at her daughter for fear she'd begun to cry. The well of her own emotional turmoil was threatening to spill over. She couldn't afford that to happen, not then.

Janine rushed into the foyer to follow Maxine. Already, Maxine had fled out onto the front steps. By the time Janine opened the door to the wicked chill of the early November air, Maxine had her arm flung through the air to hail a taxi. Janine howled her name through the escalating winds.

"MAXINE!"

What was it that made Janine want to speak with her so terribly? Why couldn't she let this go?

Janine hustled down the steps just as Maxine opened the taxi door. She hovered in the space between the door and the belly of the cab and allowed her eyes to find Janine's. They held one another's gaze for a long time. Janine would have guessed that time itself had stopped, save for the fact that cars continued to whip past, becoming streams of colors.

Before Maxine could fully tuck herself into the cab and get away, her knees knocked together again and she full-on collapsed. A wail erupted from her perfect lips. The taxi driver turned himself around and demanded something of her that Janine couldn't fully understand. Suddenly, Janine found herself there, tucking Maxine's legs tenderly into the cab, lifting her torso up so that she could sit upright. Maxine hardly seemed to realize who Janine was any longer. Janine was reminded of Maggie and Alyssa when they'd been very young and terribly tired; Jack had carried their doll-like bodies to bed, only for Janine to tuck them beneath the sheets.

Janine heard herself give the cab driver Maxine's address. She would have remembered that address on her deathbed. Heck, she still remembered Maxine's Brooklyn address and phone number, which she hadn't used in over twenty years.

"You get home safe, okay, Maxine?" Janine whispered then.

Maxine was too zonked to answer. Instead, she gripped her purse with a shaking hand and began to open it. Janine protested, thinking maybe that Maxine thought she was just another worker, waiting for a tip.

Maxine gripped something within her little clutch purse and lifted it toward Janine, nodding with finality. She pressed her fist into Janine's palm then opened it like a cracked egg over a skillet. A small metal piece fell onto Janine's hand.

"Lady, are you going to let me drive, or what?" This was the cab driver.

Janine blinked down at the half-heart connected to a shoddy metal chain. It read:

-ST

-ENDS

It echoed with memories from a far different life. She swallowed, stepped back, and then tried to get Maxine's attention again. But before she could, Maxine drew up the strength to close the door and allow the cab to take her back to her apartment alone.

There, at the edge of the sidewalk, the razor-sharp November winds threatened to take Janine down. The necklace, a relic from her past life, a silly afternoon at a mall somewhere in Brooklyn, made her heart ache. Her fingers closed over it as her conscience tried to drag her back into the service for her dead husband.

Did the necklace still mean what it had meant all those years before? Or was it now just a badly-cut piece of metal, dragged out of the bottom of a jewelry box somewhere and better off in the belly of a landfill?

# CHAPTER SIX

ALYSSA INITIALLY RESENTED Janine's request that she come back to the Vineyard after her father's funeral. "Maggie's allowed to just go back to her real life," she pointed out. "I don't see why I can't." But there was a strange green tint to Alyssa's face; her eyes seemed deeper, lost. While Maggie placed her hand tenderly on her husband's chest, tears running down her cheeks, Alyssa stood as a hard-edged, distasteful creature, her arms crossed over her chest. She seemed unwilling to face her grief, as though she thought she could jump over it in some sort of obstacle course of life. Janine had seen this reckless energy result in horrific consequences. People took to alcohol, too many sexual partners, or drugs as a way to deal with the dark void within them. If Alyssa was close, maybe she could help guide her toward therapy; heck, maybe Janine, too, could find a way to heal if one of her daughters remained near. This was a selfish thought, but it remained true regardless.

Alyssa and Janine arrived at the house on the southern edge of

Martha's Vineyard two days after the funeral. There was still so much to do back in New York. Janine had a list about a mile long—lawyers and real estate brokers to speak to, even gym memberships to cancel. Jack had belonged to nearly every sort of gym, as the upkeep of his physique had edged toward obsession.

Elsa awaited them with a large pot of coffee and a brown baggie of freshly-baked donuts from the Frosted Delights Bakery. "Jennifer sends her best," she said as she splayed out a number of glazed and vanilla-frosted and maple-stuffed donuts.

"Nothing like a carbohydrate bomb to get you through grief," Alyssa stated, her voice heavy with sarcasm.

Janine and Elsa locked eyes for a split second as Alyssa took a large bite of a glazed donut. She then sauntered toward the kitchen window, where she spotted a number of young people around a bonfire. "What's going on at the beach?"

"Cole brought some of his friends by," Elsa answered. "It's kind of a rare thing that he even wants to spend time over here. I have to admit that I don't like how much him and his pals drink. He tells me it's a sailor thing." Worry made the creases between her eyebrows deepen.

"Some of them are cute," Alyssa noted under her breath.

"Who?" Elsa feigned interest as she stepped up toward the window.

"I don't know. Maybe I like Island Boys more than I thought," Alyssa touted playfully. "Think they'll mind if I go out there and join them?"

Janine's stomach stirred. "Do you really think you should go to a party right now, Alyssa?"

Alyssa gave her mother a pointed look. "The last thing I want to do is sit around the house and mope; besides, I'm not in the city. What kind of trouble could I possibly get into?" She took another dramatic bite of her donut, grabbed her coat, then retreated into the growing darkness of the early evening as the door slammed behind her.

Janine took her place alongside Elsa and gazed out the window. Eleven people in their twenties and maybe early thirties gathered around the fire, sipping beer and snacking on processed food. A speaker blared tunes Janine couldn't quite make out. Cole greeted Alyssa warmly with a side-hug and seemed to introduce her to the others.

"My girls never had cousins before," Janine breathed.

"My kids didn't, either. It's lovely to watch them together like this."

Janine grabbed a vanilla-coated donut and took a delicate bite. Elsa stepped back and exhaled slowly, beginning a conversation about the events at the Lodge, about the next week's schedule, and about her and Carmella's little adventure on their drive back to the city, during which they'd had a flat tire. Janine could hardly concentrate. All the while, her eyes followed Alyssa as she flickered through the crowd of Cole's friends, flirting with the guys and maybe complimenting the girls, anything to get in their good graces. Alyssa and Maggie both had a flair for social interaction. It had been ingrained in their upbringing as Manhattan elites. She cracked open a beer for herself and saluted the others around the fire, who tipped their drinks toward her back. None of them could have guessed this girl had just lost her father.

"Should we have a glass of wine?" Janine heard herself ask. She needed to escape this fear, now brewing in her belly.

"I think we should," Elsa affirmed. She cracked open the fridge and discovered a half bottle of rosé, which she removed and poured into two large wine glasses. "You know, it really was a nice service," she said then, as though she thought that was what she was meant to say.

Janine didn't want to talk about Jack Potter's funeral service. She didn't want to talk about the wake afterward, where she had fallen into so many useless conversations about "how much Jack loved his daughters" and "how greatly he'll be missed." She took a long sip of her vino and closed her eyes, praying for some kind of relief. She wished Alyssa was eight again, eager to spend an afternoon on the couch with her mother.

Elsa suggested they head into the living room to cozy up under blankets. Janine resisted as she wanted to keep her eye on Alyssa. Within the space of her first few sips of wine, Alyssa cracked open her second beer on some kind of mission. Alyssa had hardly spoken on their drive back from the city, but now, she seemed to sizzle with electricity, swapping stories with everyone around the bonfire. What could she possibly say to these people? She'd been born into such a different set of circumstances. She was the granddaughter of an oil tycoon. She'd been given the world.

Now, she sauntered around a bonfire with a Coors Lite in hand like she'd never ridden half-bored in the front seat of a sports car. She'd been gifted items for random birthdays that the people around the bonfire couldn't have dreamed of.

"Maybe I'll just head out and check on Alyssa really quick," Janine heard herself say as she cleared out her own first glass of wine.

Elsa's eyes sparkled with curiosity. "She seems okay, doesn't she? Cole's watching out for her."

But Janine hardly knew Cole. In many respects, she hardly knew any of them. She stood on shivering legs and headed out onto the chilly porch, where she sauntered down the steps and then stumbled toward the sand beyond. She wasn't drunk, not after a single glass, but she felt oddly dizzy, as though the alcohol and sugar had jumped directly to her head. When she neared the fire, she caught Alyssa's gaze almost immediately as Alyssa burst into feigned laughter over a joke one of the guys had said.

"Hey! Alyssa!" Janine hated the sound of her own voice; it was overly sweet and just as fake as Alyssa's sounded. "Can I talk to you for a sec?"

Alyssa rolled her eyes flippantly, a performance for the rest of the people around the bonfire. She then dragged herself over to Janine, sipping her beer as she went.

"What, Mom?"

Janine crossed and uncrossed her arms. "Do you mind if we talk over by the house?"

Alyssa shrugged. "Why? What's up?"

"It's just that, well..." Janine spoke as softly as she could to avoid detection from this wild collection of Islanders. "I don't think it's very smart to start partying the second we get back from your dad's funeral."

The corners of Alyssa's lips quivered. "I'm just trying to loosen up."

"I know. But in the emotional state you're in, I'm worried you'll — I don't know... take it too far."

Alyssa fell into a burst of horrible, dark laughter. "I'm totally fine, Mom. You know as well as I do what Dad did. It's not like him dying is this great loss to the world, no matter how pretty Maggie put it at the funeral."

Janine's nostrils flared. Something strange and small quivered at the base of her belly. Was this the final piece of her body that remained in love with Jack Potter? Did it want to rise up and protest? What good would that do?

"I think your sister is realistic about what it means to lose him," Janine offered softly. "I think grief is a very difficult thing to process. It's like an iceberg and you're the Titanic."

"And what are you in all of this, Mom? Immune?" Alyssa's eyes caught the enormous bonfire; she looked like a beautiful demon.

"Of course, I'm not immune."

"Then why don't you turn some of these thoughts onto yourself, huh?" Alyssa countered.

Janine closed her eyes. Someone around the bonfire cracked a joke about how "hot" someone else's mom was.

"And really, it's kind of crazy that you haven't looked into more therapy for yourself since the whole thing with Maxine happened," Alyssa offered, still under her breath. "You can point the finger at me and my Coors Lite as much as you want. But there are a whole lot of spider-webs in your attic, Momma."

Janine met Alyssa's gaze for a long, quiet moment as the people around the bonfire continued on with their chatty, overly-silly conversation. Only fifteen feet away, the ocean lapped up across the sands, dark and dangerous and frothing with rage.

"Just promise me you'll be careful," she breathed.

"Mom, I'm always careful," Alyssa returned with the flip of her gorgeous tresses, already tousled by the salty ocean winds. "Just because I came back with you doesn't mean I want to be coddled. Okay?"

Janine returned to the house, refilled her glass of wine, and placed her face in her hands. Her anxiety threatened to grab hold and choke her until she couldn't breathe any longer. Elsa had suggested she order pizzas for them and Cole's houseguests. Janine thought that was a great idea and offered to pay but knew that she wouldn't find the strength to eat a greasy slice of her own. Around the time the pizza delivery driver arrived with the steamy, glorious carb-fat pizza, Henry's car appeared. Janine was three glasses of wine deep, slipping through time without much consciousness. She checked her phone and realized she'd texted him, begging him to come. Had she lost her mind?

The delivery driver entered the house with four large pizza boxes, along with six boxes of breadsticks. Janine slipped past him and met Henry on the porch. He was all bundled up, peering out from behind his glasses with eyes heavy with worry.

"Let's get back inside," he told her. "You aren't even wearing a coat."

But before he could say anything else, Janine pressed her lips upon his. His arms wrapped around her and held her tightly against him. He kissed her with an urgency and a desire she hadn't felt from a man in many, many years— not since maybe her early thirties, with Jack by her side. When their kiss broke, her cheeks were wet with tears.

"Janine," Henry breathed as he slipped a hand over her cheek. "Are you okay? I wanted to call you while you were away, but I didn't know if you'd want to hear from me."

Janine squeezed her eyes shut. The world seemed to swirl

around her. Why did she think she could care for Alyssa when she could hardly keep herself upright? She hadn't reckoned Jack's death would slice her through the belly like this.

Again, she kissed Henry, knowing all the while that it wasn't fair to put such pressure on him. She hadn't committed to him in the slightest; instead, she'd kind of strung him along, making him do everything on her pace as she dealt with the original "grief" of her breakup from Maxine and Jack. Now what? What did any of it mean?

"Janine, let's sit down for a minute, okay?" Henry whispered as their kiss broke. "Let's just talk."

"No, Henry. Let's go back to your house." Janine returned the words without thinking.

Henry was taken aback. She'd been resistant to going any further than kissing. But going back to his house implied something a whole lot more than kissing.

"No, Janine. Not tonight," Henry said initially.

But Janine's face was marred with confusion as another sob escaped. "Please, Henry. Please, take me home with you."

She just wanted someone to care for her. She wanted someone to rely on.

Henry disappeared for a moment into the house to grab her coat and, presumably, tell Elsa about their whereabouts. He then led Janine to his car, where she buckled herself in slowly, like a child who'd just learned how. He then eased the car out of the driveway and headed back to his house.

Inside, Janine perched at the edge of his bed and stared at her feet. Henry appeared with a glass of water, which he asked her twice to drink before she agreed. He sat beside her and tried to speak with her, but instead, she kissed him, wanting to forget about everything, just for a while. But mid-way through the kiss, a sob escaped her throat again. The world seemed so dark and confusing, as though everything she'd ever known could easily fall out of her grip all over again. How could she trust anything?

Henry removed the glass from her hand and placed it on the bedside table. Janine fell back and tried to collect him over her. She didn't want to verbalize her needs, didn't want to ask him to make love to her. Still, he was resistant. Something in the back of Janine's mind knew he was too much of a gentleman to do anything, especially given her current state.

Instead, Henry curled up behind her and wrapped his arms around her, spooning her. Somehow, this tenderness was overwhelming in a far different way. Janine's sobs grew louder for a full minute before she quieted again, digging herself into the cocoon of his body and slowly falling into slumber.

This was the way of Henry. This was him, giving her love and tenderness and understanding, even in the wake of so much horror. This was what Henry offered her. And when she woke the next morning, bathed in the light of the new day, she heard the soft creak of his breathing as he continued to dream on, his arms still wrapped safely around her.

# CHAPTER SEVEN

## TWENTY-FOUR YEARS BEFORE

AT NINETEEN, Janine Grimson wasn't yet married to Jack Potter when she wound up pregnant with his child. Terrified of what Jack might say but blissfully in love with him, she'd kept the pregnancy a secret for as long as she could (around eight weeks) before her bout of endless morning sickness and avoidance of alcohol tipped her hand. Jack's joy had permeated off of him like sunlight. He had leaped up from the barstool at the cocktail place they frequented, cried out the news to the multiple revelers, and then bought champagne for everyone in the establishment. Janine had been giddy with it— unbearably so, and had pinched herself with joy when she had announced it to Maxine later in a phone call.

"He wasn't upset!" Janine whispered, absolutely lost with happiness as she pressed the phone against her ear. "I don't know why but I imagined this story in my head where he took me to Jersey to get it taken care of or something. But instead, he made a lunch meeting with his mother next week to tell her everything.

Guessing she'll already know all about it since he couldn't keep his big, beautiful mouth shut at the cocktail bar."

Maxine remained in Brooklyn, another universe away from Janine's newfound life in Manhattan. She had known about the pregnancy since before that second pink line had appeared on the pregnancy stick.

Prior to this, Janine had been endlessly nervous for Jack's reaction would be. She'd only hoped deep down that he would be as ecstatic as she was and that she wouldn't have to entertain any other options. She wasn't the sort of woman to do that, for one, and for two— perhaps selfishly, she knew Jack was her ticket out of poverty.

She wasn't a gold-digger by any means. In fact, when she'd initially met Jack Potter, she'd been his waitress, a vibrant eighteen-year-old from Brooklyn ready to take on the world, making ends meet and living with her best friend in the wake of her mother's spontaneous departure from New York City. She'd been broken-hearted and overly-daring. No way in heck she would have said no to an offer of a free dinner from a handsome and rich man like Jack.

"What does this mean?" Maxine asked over the phone then. "Are you going to marry him?"

"Oh, gosh, Max, I don't know." Janine chewed at her bottom lip and caught her reflection in the antique mirror, which hung in the study of Jack's Greenwich Village apartment. Although she still paid rent at her and Maxine's place, she hadn't been there in many days.

"You will. You're going to marry Jack Potter," Maxine recited. "And you're going to be one of the richest women in Manhattan. And I'm going to rot in the gutter."

"Don't be ridiculous. You know you and me; we go everywhere together," Janine returned. Her brow furrowed as the full weight of Maxine's apparent jealousy landed upon her shoulders. Lost in the chaos of her courtship with Jack, she'd hardly envisioned what it might appear like on the other side of the East River.

---

JANINE'S BELLY wasn't exactly the kind of thing that allowed for haute-couture fashion. Now that Jack allowed her an expense account so that she could "look the part" of high-society Manhattan, Janine found it very difficult to slide herself into some of the items she yearned for the most. Jack's mother took her shopping during her fourth month for appropriate "maternity clothing," then proceeded to talk at her throughout lunch about the manner in which she was meant to behave as the next mother of the heir to the Potter fortune. Several times throughout the meal, Jack's mother referred to Janine's baby as "he." She knew better than to demand what happened if the baby they'd created was a "she."

Jack purchased an apartment on the Upper West Side, an apartment on the forty-third floor, which would suit their now-growing family. Maxine teased Janine about this, saying that now she was even too stuffy for Greenwich Village.

Janine ignored Maxine's teasings, as her love for her best friend was much greater than any kind of pettiness Maxine could offer. Midway through her fifth month, Janine dragged Maxine to one of Jack's friend's parties and watched as she canoodled her way toward a quasi-relationship with a very rich Wall Street man named Barney. Within the next two weeks, she had a four thousand dollar

Birkin Bag on her arm; by the end of Janine's seventh month, Maxine had bagged a high-paying position as an event planner at a Greenwich Village magazine. The girls were still only nineteen years old, but it already seemed as though they'd begun to "win" the game of the city.

"I wonder if they'll ever find out we're con artists," Janine had teased Maxine once over a swanky lunch at a Greenwich Village café.

"I don't know about you, darling, but I'm not faking it," Maxine had told her in an overly-wrought French accent.

Other girls' female relationships always seemed difficult, volatile. Only now, in their nineteenth year, did Janine feel the first rifts between herself and Maxine. It bruised her heart. She found herself listening to stories about Maxine amongst other of Jack's friends while she slid her hand over her belly, waiting for the Potter child to make his or her way into this world. Apparently, Maxine was up to no good all over the city— paving her way from Birkin bags to high-paying jobs to affairs with artists and beyond. Janine wasn't the sort to fling herself through men like that. She was a true believer in love. Still, she wished Maxine would reach out to her and tell her all these stories herself. She had begun to feel that Maxine wanted to one-up her so badly that she would become queen of the city and leave Janine far behind.

Even still, Janine was loyal, perhaps to a fault.

When she was eight months pregnant, Jack left for a business trip to China with his father. This left Janine terribly lonely in that high-rise apartment building all alone. She'd grown to detest the perfect view of the park; she could practically feel the laughter as it bubbled up from the grounds below, representative of countless friendships and romances, people who weren't locked in ivory towers near the clouds.

As she pressed her fingers to the glass and contemplated each and every one of her life decisions thus far, a strange thump came from her belly, followed by a twist of pain, which seemed to rocket from the base of her spine all the way to her neck. She cried out in alarm, drawing her arms around her belly. Was this what labor felt like? Wasn't it too early? She pressed her mind for the memory of what the doctor had said, but it was blank with worry and fear.

Janine tried to get Jack on the phone, but Shanghai was twelve hours ahead of New York City, which meant it was three in the morning. She paced back and forth on that high-quality, handcrafted Moroccan rug (more expensive than probably all the items in the apartments she and Nancy had shared over the years) in the living room as her anxiety mounted and the pain returned.

Finally, after an hour of swirling fear, she grabbed the phone and dialed Maxine at their old place. When she didn't pick up after five rings, she called the sculptor guy Maxine had recently run around with. The sculptor, who was from Bulgaria of all places, answered on the third ring and passed the phone off to a groggy-sounding Maxine after only a few grunted words.

"I'll be outside your door in twenty minutes," Maxine told her.

Janine had never seen a more beautiful face than Maxine's that afternoon. She pressed herself into a hug, inhaling the sultry, patchouli air of Maxine's wicked expensive perfume, remembering long-ago afternoons at perfume counters across malls in Brooklyn, when they'd only sampled the expensive items and never bought.

"Let's get you to the hospital, Momma," Maxine told her as she waved her arm in the air to hail a taxi.

Janine had thought maybe the air between them would be awkward, strained, given their friendship break over the previous months. Instead, Maxine allowed Janine to grip her hand with seemingly unlimited power with each wave of pain that passed over her.

"Have you been lifting weights?" was all Maxine joked after a particularly heinous wave.

But at the hospital, the doctor informed Janine of a horrible truth: although the baby was on its way, it would be a slow go and it was better that she leave the hospital for a while, get some fresh air, and return when things progressed. Maxine spoke to the doctor with disdain, as though she was insulted.

"Do you know who this is?" Maxine demanded. "She's giving birth to the heir to the Potter fortune."

The doctor had nearly lost all the strands of hair on his head. He scratched his nail down the center of his skull, indicating his irritation.

"I don't care if this baby's father is the pope," he retorted. "This child isn't coming for quite some time. She is only experiencing Braxton Hicks contractions. If you want to sit in a hospital room for that time, counting the minutes with your fingers, be my guest. Otherwise, go get comfortable somewhere and come back when the contractions are at least five minutes apart and gaining intensity."

"The nerve of that man," Maxine grumbled as she hailed a cab outside the hospital.

"Well, at least we know it's false labor," Janine offered.

"Yeah, well. I guess we can just hole up at your place? Wait it out?" Maxine's face scrunched slightly, a first reveal of how frightened she actually was. This was childbirth, something they hadn't yet conquered, not together or apart. It was an unexplored domain.

"I don't know. It's freaking me out lately to be in that apartment alone," Janine confided. "It's so fancy. It feels like I'm going to break something if I breathe too heavily. Plus, I don't know if you noticed, but I'm as big as a cow."

"Don't talk like that. You're glowing and you look beautiful," Maxine countered. A taxi swung over to collect them as her brow furrowed. "Okay. I think I have an idea. If you'll go along with it."

"Whatever. Just keep my mind off the fact that my life is about to change forever, maybe?"

"Deal," Maxine said.

The mid-Brooklyn dive bar The Scrapyard had been a frequent after-school hang-out spot for Janine and Maxine ever since they paid forty dollars to a guy behind a dumpster at the 711 for fake IDs. The bartender, Reggie, had known that they weren't of age, but as a Brooklyn kid himself, he had understood that even at fifteen or sixteen, you need a place to feel safe and cut loose. Poverty was a difficult thing; it wore heavily on Maxine and Janine's shoulders. The dollars they'd scraped together for beers were hard-earned but necessary.

Now, at nineteen and with a strange amount of wealth between them, Maxine and a very pregnant Janine entered The Scrapyard with a very different skip to their step. It was like walking into another dimension. Reggie, the bartender, lifted his head and gave them an immediate smile before that same smile quivered off his face just as quickly. He recognized the different air about them: probably, their clothing spoke volumes, but more than that, he'd probably heard a tale or two about the "Brooklyn Girls" who'd gotten too big for their britches. Janine began to think maybe they'd made a mistake, trying to tread on old ground. They weren't welcome.

But before she had a chance to turn back, Reggie smeared a rag over the counter, pointed his free hand toward her belly, and said, in a perfect Brooklyn accent, "You about to pop, Miss Janine."

Janine laughed outright, so much so that she collapsed into the booth she and Maxine had always shared back in high school. "I'm out for one last hurray, Reggie, and I didn't want to spend that hurray anywhere else but right here."

Reggie gave her a firm nod, an appreciation of the old times, and said, "What can I do you girls for, then?"

They ordered almost everything on the menu: fried pickles, onion rings and grilled cheeses sandwiches. Maxine ordered herself the most expensive, sugary cocktail on the menu, saying, "I always wanted to order that but never had enough cash for it." Janine ordered the same cocktail but without alcohol.

At this point, Reggie seemed to recognize he would at least make a pretty penny off of these ex-Brooklyn girls. He stirred up the perfect cocktails, dropped greasy food into the grease frier, and watched with bright eyes as they selected the next twenty songs on the jukebox— favorites from the previous few years, like Ace of Base's "The Sign," Alanis Morissette's "You Oughta Know," and Celine Dion's "It's All Coming Back to Me Now." They did this with Janine still seated and Maxine calling out the options from the jukebox itself.

If it wasn't for the enormous belly, which represented so much, Janine might have believed the two of them were sixteen again;

such was their hilarity, the sound of their laughter, and their zest for life.

Maxine lifted an onion ring and wagged it around for a moment before falling into a deep baritone, taking Janine's hand and saying, "Janine Grimson. Will you make me the happiest billionaire on earth and marry me, Jack Potter?"

Janine rolled her eyes as laughter spilled out of her. Maxine slipped the ring over Janine's finger and nodded formally. "All you have to do is give me a male heir," Maxine boomed in a deep voice reminiscent of Jack's.

"Ha," Janine breathed. "We'll see tomorrow, I guess."

Maxine grabbed another onion ring, ate it contemplatively, and then asked, "Are you scared?"

Janine's laughter faltered. "I'm terrified. Isn't it obvious?"

"It looked to me like you fell into Jack's life so well. It seemed easy for you."

"It isn't. It hasn't been."

Maxine nodded somberly. "It's not easy for me, either. All these rich men who think they own the world and want to mansplain everything to me constantly. The clothes are nice, though, and the money and the food. But..."

"I miss you," Janine said softly, interrupting.

Maxine dropped her eyes back to the greasy food between them. She wrapped her lips around her overly-sweet cocktail's straw, sucked deep, then exhaled. "I miss you, too."

"Be there with me. When my baby is born," Janine whispered.

Maxine's eyebrows lowered. "I'll be there for you with everything."

Janine lifted her chin. "Me too."

"You promise that?"

Janine lifted her pinky for a pinky swear. Just as Maxine's pinky folded over hers, labor pains ran across the front of her belly then radiated to her lower back like a slicing knife. Her eyes grew wide, then quickly shut as she gripped her belly with her free hand. She writhed with the pain, nearly snapping Maxine's pinky in two. In a moment, Maxine sprung up, wrapped her arms around her, and instructed her to breathe, breathe.

"You got this, Momma," Maxine whispered. "I'll be here with you the whole way."

When they left The Scrapyard, they left Reggie a four-hundred-dollar tip. It wasn't their money, after all, so they didn't care. Now it was time for that baby to arrive without complications, worry, or any other thoughts in the world.

# CHAPTER EIGHT

### MAXINE AUBERT

Present Day

MAXINE AUBERT hardly remembered Jack Potter's funeral. She had only glimpses of the memory, little snippets of it: stumbling down the aisle of that overwrought Cathedral, putting her Louboutins up on the back pew, slouching back, waiting for something to happen to her, anything at all, even death itself. It had felt strange, she remembered now, to see that shiny casket, knowing his body lay back in there, probably in a suit more expensive than anything her own father had ever owned. It was always anything for Jack Potter and the rest of his eternity. Had Jack Potter met his maker? Probably, he'd bought his way into heaven. That was his way.

It had been maybe a week since the funeral, although Maxine hadn't bothered to investigate any kind of calendar and had no commitment to the passage of time. She drank herself through her liquor cabinet, watched bad television, and purchased new furniture pieces that arrived at her home in a confusing array of shades and designs, none of which seemed to suit any of her rooms. She shoved each of the items into the spare bedroom, out of sight and out of mind.

That night at the nearby cocktail bar, Maxine sidled up alongside a businessman from Los Angeles, blushed her way into a first kiss, and soon brought him back to her apartment. The following day, after his departure and his promise to call her, she found that she couldn't remember his name nor what his face had looked like. Only when she pressed her face into the pillow he'd used had she any indication of what kind of man he'd been— a rich one, certainly, but forgettable and, if she remembered correctly, completely obsessed with Los Angeles in a way she couldn't comprehend. She was a New Yorker at heart. Los Angeles was just an exciting place to rub shoulders with celebrities of status, but not a place to settle down in her books.

Two nights later, Maxine found herself at a similar cocktail bar, performing a similar action. This man could have been the same one from the previous time; he also wore too much cologne. Still, the morning after, despite her best efforts, Maxine found herself with a void the size of Mississippi in her belly and a serious ache in her heart.

Alcohol couldn't fix everything. Maxine had seen enough drunks destroy themselves en route to that attempt. Still, when she asked herself what she wanted to do next, with her unlimited funds and probably forty years of life, she struggled with any answer besides, "Grab another drink." Another day passed, then another.

The blackouts became unavoidable. Maybe they were even the ultimate goal. When her consciousness edged back into view, she shoved it away with another sip of vodka. When she remembered what she'd done to Janine, she took a swig of wine. When she tried to make sense of her life, she thought long and hard about ordering drugs. Luckily, she avoided it.

Mid-November, the city lights swirled on high as she buzzed across the sidewalk, walking on jagged legs and clacking across the cement. She wore an expensive fur coat and another low-cut, glittery dress, and she walked with her head tossed back, her auburn locks swirling behind her. She heard several catcalls and milked them up as though they were her fuel. When was the last time she'd eaten? Was this an eating disorder or just a lack of commitment to living her life alone? Eating meant caring about herself. Drinking meant finding a way through the turmoil without looking at it too hard.

She came to slightly on a street corner, one that seemed drawn up from a long-ago memory. She hovered at the edge of the sidewalk and nearly teetered off of it as a taxi breezed past, honking its horn.

Somehow, she'd made it back to Brooklyn.

How was that possible? She burst into laughter at the realization. She'd avoided Brooklyn for years, trying, one-by-one, to delete the memories she had of scouring the streets for pennies and nibbling stale donuts with Janine on stoops and busted benches. But Brooklyn had changed along with everything else. It was now hipster Mecca, perhaps a place she and Janine would have flocked to back in their late-teenage years when they'd wanted to make something of themselves. Everywhere she looked, there were attractive men who wore blazers, thick glasses and spoke obstinately into headsets, as though what they said was the most important thing that had ever been spoken. She'd fallen in love with many men like that; she'd even believed their words for a while.

One beautiful, vibrant-looking girl hung on the arm of one of these spectacle-d men as they sauntered through Brooklyn together. Maxine jumped in front of her and said, "Be careful about him, honey. Just be careful. You don't know what he's capable of. Even he doesn't know what he's capable of yet."

The couple looked at her as though she had three heads. Maxine hobbled back as her stomach chilled. She was now one of those women on the streets, one she'd watched as a young girl in Brooklyn. One of those women who howled at you until you could run quickly away.

Maybe that had always been her destiny.

Somehow, Maxine found herself again in front of The Scrapyard, the dive bar she and Janine had loved in their young adult days. She froze before it as a few people entered and exited, giving her an up-down as they went. Did she dare to go in? When she pressed open the door, she found that they had redone the interior, presenting it with new wood and glass between the booths and plastic stools. Televisions hung from the corners, and everything she had remembered was now changed. Worst of all, the man behind the counter wasn't Reggie. She hadn't known how much she'd wanted to see Reggie until he wasn't there.

"What can I get for you?" The bartender scowled only slightly until she produced her Fendi purse, which was stuffed with cash. At least she could pay. It was clear from the design of her bag.

Maxine ordered herself a martini and perched on the edge of

what should have been her and Janine's old booth had they not redesigned the interior. She glared at the television screens as though they'd betrayed her. The bartender howled at the sports team, telling them to "get in the game." At this, Maxine took her first sip and wondered if ever in her life she would feel a part of the world again.

Throughout Maxine's brief time with Jack, she had learned a great deal about him that Janine had never given away. Of these, she thought of two things now. Number one: that he hated Brooklyn far more than he liked to let on, as he thought it resembled something foreign, ugly, and dirty— everything that wasn't the Potter name. Number two that he was horrific, wickedly mean, but an entirely clever man, using that wonderful vocabulary of his to articulate just how beneath him he thought you were.

Maxine sipped her martini and wavered slightly before pushing her back against the hardwood of the booth's bench. Every little dot of her spine stabbed into the back of the wood. Back when she and Janine had come here as teenagers with fake IDs, they'd eaten their weight in onion rings and fried pickles, guzzled bad beer, and flirted with twenty-something-year-olds with the kind of zeal you could only muster at sixteen. She could practically still hear their laughter as it bounced from wall to wall. "Can you girls ever give it a rest?" Reggie had asked at the time.

The game continued, and the bartender seemed to grow louder with each pass, each score. It was November, and that meant basketball, finally basketball, and he was obviously a Knicks fan, which seemed youthful and adorable to Maxine, now, especially since she'd dated so many men who'd purchased court-side seats for her. She'd even briefly dated a Knicks player, nobody ultra-famous, and found herself at a few NBA parties. During that era, she'd articulated every last party detail back to Janine, who'd had two young daughters at home and couldn't make it to every event. "Why did you marry rich if you wanted to stay home as a housewife so much?" Maxine had asked once. Janine had only laughed and said, "The money is nice, of course, but I love my husband and I couldn't stand being away from my children. I just love too much!"

Janine had given birth to Maggie after twenty hours of labor. Maxine had lived through every single one of those hours, fetching water and ice chips, allowing her fingers to be squeezed to an agonizing pulp, and watching as her best friend's face contorted into a monstrous-looking tomato with every push. When the nurse splayed Janine's little daughter across Janine's chest, just a perfect package of tiny features and jet-black hair, Maxine had felt something bigger than jealousy. She'd recognized that Janine had passed over a boundary she wasn't sure she ever would. The glow that displayed in Janine's eyes was foreign to Maxine, the sort of light Janine had never given out to her. Maxine's eyes had danced away when Janine had first nursed the baby. She'd told Janine (who'd hardly listened) that she needed a bathroom break and retreated into the bathroom to cry. Probably, she'd been overly exhausted, her body contorting and twisting with fear and shock after witnessing such a remarkable thing. Janine had brought life into the world, and for the first time, Maxine had thought about her own death.

Three or maybe four martinis later, Maxine found herself again on the streets of Brooklyn. Her feet stumbled her forward; her fingers lined the cement wall as she went forward. Did a part of her know where she was headed? She'd stopped checking in with herself and had begun to roll with the punches of whatever came next. She hardly remembered paying for her drinks at the Scrapyard. Maybe she hadn't. Maybe she'd drank her drinks and ran.

Darkness, then light. The blackouts were frequent but brief. In maybe no time at all, or maybe hours later, Maxine found herself beneath a beautiful, old but refurbished Brooklyn apartment building, one that had all the stylings of an old Manhattan building, complete with a doorman. Maxine couldn't have cared. She grabbed a stone from the ground and peered up at the windows above. She'd been to the apartment several times before and knew exactly the collection of windows to aim for. If she was even half-correct, she would smack at least one of those windows. She had to. She'd just watched a blurred version of a basketball game, for goodness sake; maybe she'd gleaned some skills.

With a sudden rush, she swept her arm upward to bring the rock skyward toward that third-floor window. Ah-ha! Remarkably, she hit it; it smacked against the glass without shattering it. Almost immediately, the doorman jumped out from his little hiding place and hollered. "HEY! What are you doing?"

Maxine stumbled back slightly and swung her arms out. Her fur coat had fallen down to her elbows, revealing her bony shoulders. She imagined herself as an icon. In reality, she was a defeated aging woman in her prime.

Just before the doorman came to fetch her, a small, familiar face appeared in the window Maxine had just thrown a rock at.

"Maggie! Maggie, it's me!" Maxine waved her arms wildly as though it was up to her to help a plane land on the runway.

Maggie pulled up the window and hollered down, just as the doorman headed outside. "Hey! Frank!"

The doorman, Frank, stopped short just before he reached Maxine.

"I'll come down," Maggie yelled. "Just bring her inside, okay?"

Maxine hobbled after Frank. Her instinct was to tell him just how stupid he would have been to take her away since she knew someone in the business. She hadn't thrown a rock against a window since she'd been, oh, seventeen? Sixteen? It made her feel alive and fired up. It reminded her of long-ago days when it had been just her and Janine against the world.

Maggie appeared in the elevator a few seconds after Maxine arrived at the foyer. The young woman, whom Maxine had just watched walk down the aisle at an outrageously expensive wedding in Martha's Vineyard ("outrageously expensive" had been Jack's words, as though he didn't buy ten-thousand dollars of scotch every now and again), did not smile when her eyes found Maxine's. She looked frightened.

"You know this woman?" Frank, the doorman, asked.

"Yes, she knows me. I was there when she was born," Maxine spat.

Maggie's nostrils flared. "I'll take it from here, Frank. Thanks a lot."

"And you'll let me know if you need anything," Frank boomed.

Back in the elevator, Maggie covered her nose for a split second, as though the alcohol smell that came off of Maxine was too strong for her precious nostrils. Maxine grumbled inwardly but couldn't articulate her own thoughts. When they reached Maggie's apartment, her husband, Rex, appeared in a pair of pajama bottoms and a college t-shirt.

"Mags? You okay?"

"Sorry. A few things happened since you fell asleep," Maggie explained as she sauntered in, her hand cupping Maxine's elbow. She then turned toward Maxine and spoke to her like a child. "What if I draw you a bath? We can put you in the guest room. Mom always stays there when she stays over."

Mom. Janine. The mere thought of her name made Maxine's stomach warm with comfort and happiness. She allowed herself to be guided like a child toward the bath, where Maggie drew water and added bubbles. In no time flat, Maxine dunked herself under, leaned her head back, and listened to the soft pop-pop of the bubbles around her.

"I just don't think we should let her stay here like that." This was Maggie's husband, Rex. Jack had approved of him, if only because he came from a typically rich Manhattan family, one he respected.

"What do you expect me to do, Rex? Throw her back on the streets?"

"She has an expensive apartment," Rex pointed out. "We could just grab her a cab and have it take her up there."

"I've known this woman since the day I was born," Maggie returned. "She looks out of her mind and clearly needs help."

"Yeah? I mean, she betrayed your mom," Rex returned. "And you still want her here?"

There was silence.

Maxine didn't want to know what Maggie would say next. She didn't want to hear a girl she loved very much throw her name under the bus. Goodness, she'd been thrown under the bus too many times, now. Most of those times had been self-inflicted.

Instead of listening, Maxine slipped her ears under the water and closed her eyes, living in the silence of the water beneath. She kept her lips slightly above the waterline to allow for oxygen, as though to prove to herself and to everyone else that she wasn't as suicidal as she truly felt.

# CHAPTER NINE

MAGGIE: **Mom! Pick up your phone!**

**MAGGIE: I don't want to explain over text.**

**MAGGIE: Okay. I'll just say— a very drunk Maxine appeared at my apartment late tonight.**

**MAGGIE: I didn't know what to do, so I put her in the guest bedroom for the night.**

**MAGGIE: Oh gosh. I wish you would pick up.**

Janine read these messages in a state of blurry shock the following morning. It was just after five, and she'd dragged herself out of bed to prep for her mother's earliest yoga class, which she'd taken to going to during the week after Jack's funeral, as she found it healed her rushing mind. Now, with the newfound information that Maxine was tucked under the cozy sheets of Maggie's guest bedroom, Janine was riddled with shock— and anger.

*How dare Maxine go to Maggie's apartment like this?*

*How dare she appear drunk and out of her mind?*

*Hadn't she torn her way through Janine's family enough?*

*Hadn't she ruined everything already?*

This wasn't a good day to deal with something like this. The thought rang through her mind with a hint of hilarity; after all, there was no such day in the history of time that prepared itself for any bit of disaster. *"Your best friend has lost her mind, gone on a bender, and appeared at your eldest daughter's apartment."* Nobody could have prepared for that.

Janine was agitated through the yoga session, so much so that she left halfway through. Her mother caught her eye as she ambled out and returned to her office. Once within, she sat cross-legged on her desk like a child and studied the schedule ahead, which involved a number of meetings with clients, all of whom had paid good money for her services at the Katama Lodge. It was now six-forty-five and still probably too early to call Maggie, who normally awoke around seven-thirty. Still, she couldn't wait any longer.

Maggie answered on the third ring. Her voice was groggy but edged with anxiety, reminiscent of her childhood voice.

"Mom?"

"Hi, honey." Janine tried her best to sound stable and not like the woman who'd also lost her mind over the summer in the wake of Jack and Maxine's betrayal. "Is Maxine still with you?"

"She's still sleeping, I think," Maggie replied. "Mom, she looked so panicked. I don't know if she understood where she was. I've never seen her like this before. And the smell... It was unbelievable."

Janine closed her eyes. Was this really the direction life went? You lived. You loved. You fell apart.

"Are you going to work today?"

"Rex and I are both working from home today," Maggie explained. "We can keep an eye on her. Make sure she gets home okay."

"I would come to the city right now if I could, but I have a ton of appointments. I've taken off too many days at this place the past few weeks. I need to catch up on everything."

"I understand, Mom," Maggie affirmed, her voice growing more powerful. "I promise you. We'll be okay here."

Janine forced herself through her first batch of appointments, women who explained they'd "lost their way," or "couldn't stop eating chocolate," or "felt they would lose their minds over the redesign of their living room." Janine did her best to give them the attention they'd come here to seek. Unfortunately, however, her mind was heavy with her own worries. She could only picture the haggard Maxine she'd helped into the taxi at Jack's funeral. She could only imagine a future in which she'd learned that Maxine had died of alcohol poisoning— a future in which she would regret every day she hadn't done something more to help her.

At lunch, Janine called Alyssa to check-in. Things had been strange between them since they'd arrived back from the funeral. Alyssa had spent the previous few days with Mallory or Cole and avoided her mother at all costs, only checking in to say goodnight before she went to sleep.

Alyssa didn't answer her phone, and her text messages went to only a single checkmark. Janine felt riddled with doubt. She headed into the foyer to check on Mallory, who worked at the front desk of the Katama Lodge.

"Hey Mal," she said, using her friendliest tone, which rang false in her own ears. "Any idea where my daughter might be today?"

Mallory removed her pen from her lips and turned her eyes toward Janine's. "Huh. You know, I think she said something about going out sailing with some of Cole's friends?"

Janine remembered that crew out on the beach, none of whom she could have said she approved of if it was up to her to say such a thing. She was fearful they would distract her with reckless island partying and sailing expeditions. Distract her from what, Janine wasn't entirely sure. Her true "goals" in life, whatever those were? Did anything like that matter any longer?

"What's up?" Mallory studied Janine's face as her eyebrows stitched together. "Are you worried about her?"

"No, no," Janine replied, clearly distracted. "I just hope she's not too cold. Sailing in November isn't the warmest. You couldn't pay me to do that." She then shuffled off down the hallway, muttering to herself.

En route back to her office, she passed by her mother, who placed a hand on Janine's shoulder to stop her gently. Janine blinked up, genuinely shocked at the sight of her.

"You look like a little lost pup," Nancy told her.

Janine couldn't help it. The words spilled out from her lips. "Maxine showed up at Maggie's house last night. She said that Maxine seemed out of her mind."

All the color drained from Nancy's face. She beckoned for Janine to enter her own office, where she latched the door closed and watched as Janine collapsed on her couch, her eyes toward the water beyond the window. Nancy remained standing. She collected the tips of her fingers together near her chest as she contemplated through the silence. Janine still wasn't accustomed to her mother coming up with practical solutions; she wasn't waiting for one.

"Have you talked to her?" Nancy finally asked.

"Yes, I spoke with Maggie this morning."

"I don't mean Maggie. I mean Maxine."

Janine drew her head around to meet her mother's gaze. "I don't have a whole lot to say to Maxine, Mom."

Nancy nodded somberly. "I understand that."

Janine remembered the piece of friendship necklace that Maxine had slipped onto her palm when she'd been so drunk and out of her mind that she hadn't been able to stay upright at an official, Godforsaken funeral.

"You've done a lot of forgiving this year, Janine," Nancy started then as she splayed her hands over her thighs. "You came back to me. We've become— well, I hope to say, friends."

Janine met her mother's gaze again. "We are friends, Mom. I think we're even more than that now." She was surprised at the finality and seriousness of her tone.

"I'm not saying that you have to forgive Maxine. Not in the slightest," Nancy continued. "I'm just thinking of what we stand for here at the Lodge. We see women from all walks of life, women who've made enormous mistakes, women who struggle day-in and day-out to mend the horrible things they've done."

Janine's lips parted in surprise. "You're not suggesting that we bring Maxine here? To the Lodge, are you?"

Nancy remained silent as the suggestion swam through the air between them.

"Mom, that's crazy," Janine insisted then. "After all Maxine put me through? After all I've been through just in the previous five months? I've hardly healed myself."

"And isn't that part of what we stand for here at the Lodge?" Nancy countered. "That we'll never truly be healed? That life is a process, a hunt for that very idea?"

Janine's eyes widened with annoyance. "I can't imagine extending this offer to her. And why would she even accept it? She wouldn't. It's just too much. It's too—"

"Ask yourself, Janine. Why did Maxine go to Maggie's place of all the apartments in New York City?" Nancy breathed as she held her daughter's stare.

"I don't know. I don't know. I've asked myself that very question every minute since I woke up," Janine whispered. She brought her fingers to her eyes and pressed her eyelids hard until she saw only darkness and bright yellow spots.

"I know for a fact her parents are dead. She doesn't have any siblings," Nancy continued tentatively. "Does she have anyone else in the world? Anyone else other than you?"

"She really should have asked herself that before..." Janine retorted before stopping herself.

"I know, honey," Nancy whispered. "I can't tell you what to do."

Janine returned to her office. Her head felt about as heavy as a bowling ball, apt to roll off her neck and onto the floor. She hovered at the window and peered out at Katama Bay, which whipped to-and-fro with the wild November winds. Did Alyssa really lust after such a treacherous day at sea? This was a far cry from the little Manhattanite girl Janine had raised. Perhaps this was proof of an adventurous side. Perhaps this was necessary for her future development.

Janine exhaled all the air from her lungs, lifted her phone, and dialed a number she'd deleted from her phone back in May. Back then, she'd apparently been under some idea that she would eventually forget the number she'd burned into the back of her mind in case of emergency. She hadn't gotten so lucky.

The phone rang four times. Each ring felt deeper, more powerful, as though each one demanded more of Janine's soul. She remained standing, her hand shaking against her thigh, until finally, finally, a very sober, very clear, slightly French-accented voice answered.

"Hello."

Janine was genuinely shocked at this exchange. She'd called this number more than a million times. Normally, the women charged into a hilarious conversation, with countless stops and starts and bursts of laughter. Normally was not now.

"Hello," Janine echoed. "I heard that you um. I heard you..."

"I checked myself into a psychiatric facility," Maxine replied then. "What I did last night was the last straw. How dare I bring your daughter into things? I love that girl. I want her to have the world. And I never wanted any of this to happen."

Janine's lips parted in genuine shock. Was this conversation actually happening?

"Which facility are you in?" Janine breathed.

"It doesn't matter, Jan," Maxine told her, her voice firm. "I just want to say this. I don't know what I would have done without you. At age ten, I met you. And on my deathbed, I will dream of you.

You were the love of my life. I will never forgive myself for what I did to you and your family. Now, he's gone. And Janine—"

Here, Maxine allowed herself to sob just once.

"Janine, why didn't you tell me he was so cruel? He must have been so cruel to you. He was so abusive, Janine..."

Janine's eyes closed quickly as a tear rolled down her cheek. Jack had changed significantly during her mid-thirties as life disappointment and unrest had fallen over him. She hadn't known what to do. She'd tried every trick in the book. Still, he belittled her wrinkles, her fashion, her family name, her Brooklyn origins, everything.

"In the few months I dated him, I never thought I was good enough," Maxine breathed.

Janine let out a strange laugh. She hardly recognized it. "And maybe in all the years I was married to him, I thought the same thing."

They held the silence for a moment. Janine felt her heart might explode in her chest. Finally, she whispered, "Let me talk to your doctor, Max."

"You really don't have to do that."

"Please, I'm your next of kin, aren't I? Your emergency contact?"

Maxine's laughter was so low that it was difficult to discern. "I never changed it."

"Neither did I."

# CHAPTER TEN

ELSA AND CARMELLA squabbled in the kitchen over what to cook for dinner. Bruce and Cody both planned to join them within the hour, and said that they didn't care what the women made, as long as it was hot and ready upon their arrival. Carmella wanted something simple, a stew with the freshly-baked bread she'd picked up from the Sunrise Cove Bistro, while Elsa wanted something with a bit more "oomph" to it, something that would impress Bruce, who was a bit newer to the equation and more impressionable.

"Cody and I literally just started dating. Are you suggesting that I shouldn't make him stew?" Carmella demanded with a hint of sarcasm.

"It's not that. It's just you two have been best friends for years. You probably ate French fries off of his car floor together, knowing you two," Elsa retorted.

Carmella turned her eyes into the back of her skull. "Okay,

again, if you're so picky, why don't you select what we make? I'm all ears and ready to chop."

"Like I would give you a knife when you're this annoyed with me," Elsa returned with a crooked grin. She then turned toward Janine, who stood like a ghost at the window, gazing out across the windswept beaches. "Any help, Janine? You know me and Carmella could argue about this all night, given the chance."

Janine lifted a finger and pointed out the window, clearly distracted. Yet again, Alyssa had gathered with Cole's friends along the waterline for a vibrant bonfire. Alyssa's laughter churned through the volatile air. She slumped against a man in his mid-to-late twenties, a beer in hand, and curled her lips toward his ear to whisper something. Janine's stomach burned with fear.

"Who is that guy Alyssa's wrapped around like a tree?"

Carmella and Elsa hustled on either side of her to peer out the window. Elsa made a strange noise in the base of her throat.

"That's Luuk," Elsa said finally. "Spelt L-U-U-K. He's from the Netherlands, apparently. He arrived on the island last summer or the one before it? I'm not even sure he's legally allowed to live in the United States."

Janine's nostrils flared. "You're kidding."

"Cole says he's a fantastic sailor and a whole lotta fun, which aren't two things I attribute to entirely good people," Elsa continued as she headed back toward the counter to remove a large pot, presumably for stew, as she hadn't come up with any other idea on her own. "He has a small apartment near the sailing club, which he sleeps in for free in return for giving sailing lessons to tourists and keeping the place clean."

Janine dropped her head back as frustration brewed at the base

90

of her belly. "Alyssa's doing that little dance of hers. I've seen her do it since kindergarten, I swear. Her little crushes on the other little boys always seemed to manifest this future where she would run around the city, hopping from guy to guy."

Elsa drizzled olive oil into the base of the pot and clucked her tongue contemplatively.

Carmella interjected before Elsa could finish her thought. "Your daughter is a good girl. I'm sure she's just trying to blow off some steam. Who amongst us hasn't wanted to just flirt with a stranger and pretend everything's all right?"

"Speak for yourself." Elsa countered.

"Okay, Elsa, we get it. You're Miss Perfect and the rest of us fall short," Carmella said as she stabbed a knife through an onion with force.

"He got into a bit of legal trouble maybe this past summer," Elsa continued, as though Carmella hadn't said anything at all. "Seems like he was sailing drunk? Cole thought he was going to get deported. Maybe he knows the right people."

Along the waterline, Alyssa cracked open another domestic beer as this Luuk fellow wrapped his massive Dutch arms around her and lifted her in a wild circle, one that sprayed beer across the sands. Alyssa's shriek bellowed up out of the sound of the howling winds.

Janine countered this with a pour of her own glass of wine. Carmella and Elsa continued their useless squabble as her thoughts dug themselves deeper into shadows. She tip-toed around her worry for Alyssa as Maxine's doctor's words found her again. "If she hadn't come to us sooner, I feel very certain she would have found a way to take her own life," he'd explained to her. "She was malnourished and on a very serious alcohol bender. She couldn't articulate her thoughts very well upon her arrival. But now, we have her on light foods, things like soup and crackers, and her eyes have brightened. If you like, I'm sure you could come in to visit her soon."

There was the rush of the front door then the clink of a pair of keys in the little bowl in the foyer. The sound of Nancy's gait brought her all the way to the kitchen, where she beamed at the three of them. "I've started to feel like everything's about to calm down," she said after her girls greeted her. "After the health scare and the hurricane and Jack's death and the wedding... It's been a whirlwind. I don't know about you, but I'm about ready to stuff myself with Thanksgiving dinner and rest till spring."

"We're hardly able to agree on what to make for dinner tonight," Carmella offered. "I don't know how we'll get through Thanksgiving."

Nancy sidled up alongside Janine and passed her a glass of chardonnay. Her eyes followed Janine's out toward Alyssa, where she swung an arm over the broad chest of the Dutch sailor as though she claimed him.

"Feels like I made a mistake bringing Alyssa here," Janine murmured.

"No. It's all going to be okay," Nancy breathed. "She feels the come-down I just spoke about. She wants to breathe again. Maybe we should all take a note from Alyssa."

"Drink cans of beer on the sand?" Carmella teased.

"Something like that, with a little more French flair," Nancy offered with a slight tip of her wine glass.

"I just worry she'll forget all the things she always wanted," Janine tried then, unwilling to drop the subject completely.

"Darling, think about yourself," Nancy said then. "You didn't pull your career together until much later in life."

"Yes, but I had to work hard for what I had..." Janine replied softly. "I couldn't just run around like—"

What she wanted to say here was: like a trust fund kid. But actually, both her daughters were that. She'd arranged that life for them.

"Well, until you were nineteen," Nancy continued. "Younger than Alyssa. When you gave birth to Maggie and everything changed."

Janine's throat tightened. She couldn't make her worry understood. Old resentment stirred as she sipped more wine and made her way back into the dark shadows of the house. How could Nancy possibly understand? She'd left Janine in New York at eighteen. Janine had been in free-fall when she'd met Jack, a hungry waitress with an enormous will to live.

"If she hadn't come to us sooner, I feel very certain she would have found a way to take her own life." The doctor's words hummed through her mind once more.

She should have taken Maxine aside the day of the funeral. She shouldn't have allowed any of this to happen. Didn't they have a responsibility to hold one another up? To be there for one another after all the pain and hurt they'd gone through. Janine had to question her resolve and if she could be there for her.

Janine's phone buzzed with a call from Henry. She hadn't seen him since her spontaneous and uneventful sleepover at his place, which had complicated things between them greatly. She worried that the fact that they'd just slept had made Henry think that all she really wanted from him was friendship. She worried that because she hadn't reached for him, maybe all she would ever be ready for was friendship. How could anyone be sure they were ready for love? It was never the right time.

"Hey!" Henry's voice was warm, inviting. "How have you been?"

Janine hated this question, as it seemed to point at the fact that she hadn't texted, hadn't called. They'd been in a kind of holding pattern, watching one another on their opposite sides of the island as the winds howled around them.

"Oh, good. Fine." These words simmered with lies. "And you?"

"Pretty okay," Henry told her.

Silence. Did she know this man at all? He could have been a telemarketer.

"I was wondering if you wanted to have dinner tonight," Henry continued.

"Oh."

In the kitchen, Elsa screeched that Carmella had come too close to her with the vegetable knife. Carmella retorted that she was forever a drama queen, no matter the occasion. Nancy's laughter howled between them. Even they seemed foreign to Janine.

"But don't worry if you don't have time," Henry broke the silence just then. "I know you've been through a lot."

"I can meet you," Janine finally replied. Her heart cracked at the edges, imagining a dark and shadowed dinner conversation, wherein she couldn't think of anything worthwhile to say at all. "Maybe around eight?"

# CHAPTER ELEVEN

"LISTEN, Henry. I'm still married to a dead man. My best friend is half out of her mind at a psychiatry facility. My daughter's on a quest to ruin her life." Janine gripped the steering wheel of her car as she hovered in the darkness outside of the Edgartown Fish Shack, the restaurant Henry had spontaneously requested. "There's just a whole lot on my mind right now. And when you held me all night long..." She trailed off, too embarrassed even to say the words to herself. It was funny how far you could go with something— your emotional journey, your bravery and still feel like you hadn't moved an inch, that you were still at the base of the mountain, looking up at the immense travel ahead.

Henry appeared at the front tip of her car. He wore a thick winter coat with an orange knitted hat, probably something he'd tugged out of his mother's front closet, something previously worn a hundred or a thousand times. He gave her a sturdy wave. Janine hopped into the chill and shut her car door closed. They hovered a few feet away from one another, assessing each other like opponents might before a tennis match.

"I like the hat," Janine complicated with a smile.

"Oh, thank you." Henry's cheeks burned crimson as he tugged it off. "I found it at my mother's house. I wanted to look the part of a silly middle-aged man who didn't care about his fashion sense."

"What has this island done to you, Henry? You've lost that cynical New York City fashion sense," Janine grinned, grateful she could trust herself to make the slightest of jokes.

"The artist community in Greenwich Village has already sent me a warning letter for a knitted sweater I wore last week," Henry explained as they assembled themselves along the walkway that led to the bustling restaurant beyond. "I wanted to ask you. You didn't tip them off, did you?"

Janine's laughter was genuine, broad, and almost unrecognizable. "Henry, I don't make the rules, but I do like to uphold them."

"Shoot. I knew it," Henry replied. "I never should have trusted you."

These last words rang overly true. They sliced through Janine's stomach as her smile faltered. By then, they reached the front door, which Henry pulled open, his face stitched into a scowl of his own. By the time they reached their assigned table, they'd fallen again into the dull creak of silence, made all the worse with the contrast from the vibrant conversations swirling from all corners.

What could Janine tell him? She pondered this as she tried to study her menu, but her thoughts took over once again. *Henry, you've been a welcome reprieve from a horrible year. Henry, I want you in my life as much as possible— but I don't know what that looks*

*like for either of us. Henry. Henry. Just the sound of your name*
*makes me shiver with longing. Henry...*

Henry ordered them a bottle of wine. Afterward, Janine lifted
her eyes and realized he was now studying her contemplatively.

"Do you know what you want to order?" she asked him, if only
because that's what you were meant to ask at restaurants.

"A slot opened up in the Lisbon Film Festival," he said instead.
"My documentary is being featured."

Janine's lips parted in shock. Selfishly, foolishly, she hadn't
envisioned this evening going in this direction.

"Congratulations," she whispered before shaking her head
violently and coming up with a second, much louder,
"Congratulations!"

"Yes, thank you. It's been a whirlwind," Henry answered. "I
didn't think I'd gotten into any of the major European festivals. I
was bummed, to say the least."

"Wow. When is it?" Janine could at least pretend she wanted to
go and then think about it beforehand.

"Actually, I have to leave in the morning," Henry replied
delicately.

"Oh!" So actually, Janine wasn't invited. Actually, Henry
hadn't really included her in the plans at all. Could she blame him?
She'd given him no indication that she wanted his love.

"But there's more," Henry continued.

"Wow. More than a film festival in Portugal?"

Henry shifted his weight. "I've been asked to help a friend on a
project in China."

"Goodness. China." Janine had a funny internal laugh; after all,
that's where Jack had been when Maggie was born. What was it

about that massive country? It seemed to have so much weight in her life.

"Yes, I know. It's pretty exciting," Henry fiddled with his napkin as he held eye contact.

The waiter arrived to pour them two glasses of wine. Janine lifted her glass to clink with his. "Congratulations on both fronts."

Henry's eyes reflexed a storm of different emotions. "I would leave directly from Portugal to head out to China."

"That sounds exciting." Janine took a long sip of her wine. "Well, I guess I should have known that your time on the island was limited." Henry had only come back to make sense of the place in the wake of his mother's death. He'd grown up there; he was connected to generation after generation of islanders, including the many lighthouse keepers at the Edgartown Lighthouse.

"Janine..." Henry began softly.

"I'm so excited for you," Janine blurted as her voice wavered the slightest bit, so she focused her gaze on the glass of wine before her. "It must be remarkable to be called all over the world to work on these projects. You're so talented, Henry. Really."

The waiter arrived to take their food order. Janine forgot what she'd said the moment the waiter left them behind. There was something behind Henry's eyes, a hesitation Janine couldn't understand. Why had he wanted to tell her this over dinner? It felt like a breakup. It felt like finally, Henry had decided he wanted to break free of her and her poisonous affection for him.

"It's been so wonderful getting to know you, Janine," Henry said softly.

Janine's eyes welled with tears. "Oh, gosh. I don't mean to be dramatic. We'll see each other when we see each other. You'll be back on the island every now and again, won't you?"

"Sure," Henry offered with a flippant shrug of his shoulders. "I'll be around."

Janine wanted to demand how often. Once a year? Every six months? But she knew you couldn't ask that of anyone. It was rude and intrusive. She'd never been direct about her needs with him because she'd never known her needs. And now, he'd recognized his own needs to be somewhere on the other side of the earth. She had to respect that.

"You're going to be so successful," Janine said then. "The documentary world won't know what hit them."

"I do think there are so many stories to tell," Henry continued. "So many people I want to meet. So many places I want to go to. The only worry I have, sometimes, is that I'll propel myself into everyone else's stories without ever making sense of my own story. Who is Henry Dawson, anyway?"

"Who are any of us?" Janine countered.

"Good point. Now you sound like a therapist," Henry returned with a laugh.

Janine wished she could hold onto the sound of that laugh; she wished she could live within it, as though it was a kind of cave.

"Phew, Henry. It's been a whirlwind of a few months, hasn't it?" Janine tried. Maybe she could sound normal. Maybe she could sound like someone people recognized as sane.

"You can say that again," Henry affirmed.

Janine forced herself to eat a decent amount of salmon and drink one and a half glasses of wine, enough so that Henry thought of her as "normal." She then paid, saying, "I insist, Henry. We're celebrating your success," and followed him out into the parking lot, where they hugged for a final time, avoided any kissing, and parted ways.

Henry took the exit and disappeared into the darkness of the all-consuming November night.

This left Janine to finally lose control inside her car.

She pounded the steering wheel as tears streamed down her cheeks. A strange hollowness opened up in her belly. How easily she'd placed Henry within her heart! How easily she'd fallen for him! He'd shown her a side of the island and a side of herself she'd never envisioned. He'd been her balm after the worst burns of her life. He'd been her summer rain.

*"Not everything can last forever, Janine,"* she told herself now, trying to lift herself up. *"Your daughters got older. Your marriage ended. You even left the city you said you'd never be caught dead living outside of. You're different. You have to allow other people to change, too."*

But Janine's heart was battered and bruised. She closed her eyes and again found herself staring at the image of Jack's coffin, lowered into the ground to wait out eternity. Alyssa had nearly fallen at the sight of it. Maggie had struggled to keep her upright. Janine wished you could go into your brain and delete images like this; the memory of Jack's burial wouldn't serve any purpose later. It would only bring sorrow.

Maxine, alone in a psychiatric ward.

Maxine, in the wake of a horrible mental shift.

This was the same Maxine who had helped Janine cheat on her science test in eighth grade after Nancy had stayed up all night screaming at her boyfriend, not allowing Janine to study. This was the same Maxine who'd always been there to lend an ear, give her moral support and just be the best friend a girl could have. Nobody could replace her. This was the same Maxine who'd suggested she was brave enough and beautiful enough to always get what she wanted.

Janine cleared her calendar for the next two days. They'd recently hired another part-time naturopath doctor to fill Janine's spot, especially in the midst of the confusion with Jack's death and Janine's arrangement of the funeral and burial. This doctor could handle her appointments here and there over the next few days. The Lodge would carry on.

It was nearly ten— the final ferry left from Oak Bluffs at ten-fifteen. Janine sped over to that little cozy cove of colonial homes and quaint restaurants. Once there, she purchased a vehicle ticket and eased her car up onto the ferry, where she stepped out of the car and stomped up to the top deck. Up there, she purchased a cup of coffee and a croissant, brain food for the journey ahead. She would drive as long as she could.

**MAGGIE: Just text when you're here, no matter the time. It's not like I can sleep much these days anyway.**

# CHAPTER TWELVE

THREE IN THE morning on a street corner in Brooklyn. Janine hovered at the edge of the sidewalk and imagined herself, a strung-out Maxine, hunting for a rock to fling at the window. How had she even remembered which one belonged to Maggie? Maxine had been to Maggie and Rex's apartment a handful of times, but that had all been in another reality, another time so long ago. Janine could only imagine herself saying such simple things like, *"What restaurant should we go to for lunch?"* Or, *"Please, Maxine, are you ever going to tell me where you got that sweater?"* You could never peel back the layers of time and return to the past. You were always thrust out, alone and afraid, on a street corner in Brooklyn in the middle of November.

The doorman recognized Janine as Maggie's mother. Janine gave him a tip and thanked him for his help regarding the woman who'd come for Maggie. The doorman told her, simply, that it was his job to care for the residents of the building.

When Janine reached her floor, Maggie leaped out from behind her apartment door and allowed herself to be completely enveloped in her mother's arms. A sob escaped her lips. Janine held her eldest daughter's head tenderly and blinked as she continued to hold her. A pizza sat on the counter of the kitchen, untouched save a piece or two and just beyond the doorway, Rex slept soundly on the couch, as though he'd promised to stay up with Maggie but hadn't quite made it. Janine had made it, though; she'd floundered through her own life, cried through the cold, dark night, and now, here, with Maggie in her arms, she was needed.

The click of the door closing made Rex erupt from the couch. He wiped his fingers over his eyes and hurriedly brewed them hot water in preparation for hot cocoa.

"He thinks he's invented the perfect recipe," Maggie informed her mother as they folded their legs up on the couch. On the coffee table, a book was open to save the page. The book was titled, *You Lost Your Dad. Now What?* Janine wondered why so many book titles had to be styled as though they were silly blog articles.

"Oh. That." Maggie quickly gripped the book, closed it, and slipped it under her couch. "The self-help section of the bookstore recommended it."

"I understand," Janine tried. "Has it helped at all?"

"Not really. Although there's a whole section about how to deal with your father's death if your father also happened to be a world-class a - hole." She dropped her eyes to her thighs, muttering. "Sorry, but he was."

Janine's stomach curdled. Rex appeared with two piping-hot mugs of hot cocoa and placed them gently on two coasters, expensive ones they'd received for their wedding. Janine wanted to say something commonplace and easy, like, how wasn't it wonderful that Jack had been around for Maggie's wedding? Instead, she sipped her hot cocoa, which coated the back of her tongue and immediately burned it. Great.

Rex retreated to their bedroom to allow them mother-daughter time alone. Maggie asked about Alyssa, saying, "She's been updating her social media with all these photos of people I've never seen before."

"Yes. Cole introduced her to his friends." Janine swallowed the lump in her throat. "Everyone tells me to lay off her and just give her some space, to let her breathe. I'm just worried she's headed toward some kind of breakdown. Can you talk to her? Maybe just check-in."

"You know Alyssa doesn't like to be told what to do," Maggie murmured. "She'll sometimes do the opposite. She's like Grandma Nancy in that way."

Janine nodded. "I'm sure I had my own wild streaks back in the day. Probably a lot of that happened after Grandma Nancy left the city and I felt really, really alone. I want Alyssa to know I'm there for her if she needs me. I just—" She shook her head as her heart dropped into her stomach.

Maggie studied her. "It was strange, having Maxine here."

Janine looked at her daughter with sorrow in her eyes and finally shook her head. "I can't even imagine, honey."

"It was strange in a way I couldn't have guessed," Maggie continued. "Because when I first saw her, I wasn't afraid. In my heart of hearts, instinctively, I think of her as an extension of you. So I peered down into the dark night, saw Maxine, and felt like everything was going to be all right. I can't explain it."

"She's very sick," Janine breathed.

"Yes. She is." Maggie took a long sip of cocoa. "But she's not too far gone. Thin, yes. Frightened, yes. Alone in the world? Well. I don't know about that."

"I don't know, either," Janine murmured.

"Nobody would blame you if you never spoke to her again," Maggie assured her mother.

Janine let out a long breath. "I know that."

The corners of Maggie's lips quivered. "But you would blame yourself. Wouldn't you?"

"I don't know. I came to the city to think. It's a funny thing. It's the opposite of what I've always done. The city is a colossal burning energy; it's an ever-present, churning thing. When you're in the midst of it, you can run yourself ragged, just trying to keep up with it. I felt that way before I met your father, and I felt that way into my early forties. But now..."

Now that Henry left. Now that everything seemed in flux. Now that up was down and sideways was a whole other dimension. Now, she didn't know anything at all.

"I just wanted to walk my old streets with my darling girl," Janine continued, trying to rebound. "And try to make sense of the world I built for myself. The one your father, gave me. The one I brought you girls up in and how different it is from the one I once knew."

Maggie's eyes grew shadowed. "It's difficult for me to think about, sometimes. Especially living back in Brooklyn, which is so gentrified now. You and Grandma Nancy... You had nothing. The poverty in these streets... The people struggling to get by... And the people who've had to leave the city, just because they couldn't make ends meet any longer. It's alarming."

It was nearly four. Janine stepped toward the window and peered out at the dark and ragged sidewalk outside. A cop car blinked its red and blue lights menacingly, kitty-corner from Maggie's building. When Maggie and Rex had first moved in, Jack had put up a hissy fit and demanded why they needed to live in Brooklyn, of all places. Janine had resisted the sting of his words, telling herself Jack simply wanted nothing but the best for her daughter. Wasn't that what she wanted, too?

Maggie's eyelids hung low. Janine hustled over to grab the mug of hot cocoa from her hands before the dense, hot liquid spilled over the glow of her porcelain legs. Maggie buzzed her lips, annoyed with herself.

"I want to stay up and talk," she whispered.

"Don't worry about that. We'll have plenty of time to talk in the morning."

Twenty minutes later, after Janine had pierced through Maggie's collection of lotions and creams, she dove into one of Maggie's overly-large sleep shirts. Janine slipped herself between the recently-changed sheets of Maggie's guest bed and nestled against the feather-down pillow. The police lights continued to swirl against the edge of the windowsill, casting their ominous lights across the floor. As a child, she and Nancy had lived in the midst of crime and loud noises and screaming police sirens. This wasn't her world any longer. She rose and drew the curtains, grateful for her ability to sleep but also guilty about it.

Maggie took her mother to the most "sensational" new brunch restaurant in Bushwick, a place she termed a "social media guru's paradise" and a killer place for an oversized plate of blueberry pancakes and mimosas. Janine, who'd come spontaneously to the city she loved in the clothes she'd worn to her dinner with Henry, showered and dressed in one of Maggie's longer, floral skirts, along with a thick sweater, her coat, and the shoes she'd come in.

"I don't look like a forty-three-year-old woman pretending to be a twenty-four-year-old Brooklyn woman, do I?" she asked Maggie sheepishly as Maggie finalized her lip gloss.

"What? No." Maggie gave her mother an up-down as she capped her gloss. "You look stunning. Really. Maybe you should even take that skirt. I almost never wear it."

Did that mean the skirt was ugly or last year's style? Janine's stomach lurched at the idea that she was out of sight, out of mind, out of touch. But Maggie blew those thoughts from her mind, swept her arm through Janine's, and marched out into the streets that swam with perfect autumn-in-the-city fashion.

"Remember when everyone in the city wore those Ugg boots?" Janine asked, genuinely impressed with the season's looks.

"Ugg boots? Hmm. I think I had a pair of those when I was, what, ten?" Maggie asked with a laugh.

"You were always on the forefront of New York City fashion," Janine teased.

"Oh, come on. You and Maxine always knew what was up. Me and Alyssa used to watch you two get ready for the outings you guys would attend. Trying on ten to fifteen different outfits, having your stylist do your hair. Laughing yourselves silly over champagne." Maggie shrugged slightly, sensing maybe she'd said too much.

But in the silence that followed, Janine breathed, "No. I like it when you talk about it. It reminds me of this tremendous love Maxine and I have between us. And that we shouldn't have ever allowed anything to break our bond."

They ordered a breakfast fit for a king: a six-inch stack of blueberry pancakes, bacon that zinged with greasy crunch, English muffins, cheeses, honey, fresh eggs cooked over-easy so that their bright yellow yolk seemed like a miracle as it dripped from the heart of them. They ordered a pitcher of mimosas and filled their glasses high with orange bubbles.

To Janine's surprise, Maggie spoke about her first few weeks as a married woman with beautiful and poetic articulation. It seemed that she had a number of thoughts about what it meant to align yourself with one man for the rest of your life (which was the hope), and she felt unafraid to translate these thoughts to her mother as they slathered honey over their buttery English muffins.

"So many of my friends scoffed at the idea of me marrying Rex. They said it isn't a modern thing anymore, marrying yourself off. They asked me how I could possibly know he was the one, you know?"

Janine nodded somberly. How had she known Jack was "the one" or "the one at the time"? She'd already birthed his babies; he had a foolish amount of money in the bank; plus, at the time, and for many years after, she loved him to bits. It had been enough.

"I told them I didn't know anything," Maggie continued. "I told them that we can't possibly see the future. But I told them I wanted to dare myself to remember how much I love him now, every day for the rest of my life. And maybe that paperwork is an obsolete idea, but it still links me to that day when I felt almost just an inch away from being one hundred percent sure. Now, we've settled back into our lives together at the same apartment we've lived in for years. But it feels more stable. More settled. I know that if he leaves a sponge in the sink, I probably won't pack up my suitcase and head to the Vineyard. He knows that if I get overly dramatic about something, he won't leave me here, either. We'll compromise. We'll talk. And we'll get better at it as the years go by. At least, that's my hope."

Maggie turned her eyes to her half-eaten egg and ticked the edges of her tongs into the soft goop. "And Mom?"

Janine lifted her chin with surprise at the tenderness with which Maggie spoke. "What is it?"

Maggie's eyes brimmed with tears. "I think I already want to try. To get pregnant, I mean."

Janine's heart swelled. She brought her hand over Maggie's free one and gripped her fingers.

"I don't want to make any mistakes," Maggie rasped.

Janine chuckled as the first of many tears fell from her eyes. "Well, I hate to break it to you, honey. But you're bound to make a whole lot of mistakes. I know I did. And I know I still will. Our fallibility makes everything a little more beautiful, don't you think? It means we have to forgive. It means we have to grow beyond our wounds. It means..."

She faltered for a moment. Off to the side of a restaurant, two young mothers in their mid-twenties held babies against their chests and spoke in hushed whispers. Both wore the newest, trendiest line of Brooklyn-artistic fashion, with handy towels splayed over their chests to ensure their babies didn't spit up. The women seemed captivated with one another, so much so that they struggled to keep their whispers quiet.

"I'd help you if you want to leave him," the brunette one hissed.

"I just don't know what—"

"No. Listen to me and then listen to yourself," the brunette countered. "We have to hold one another up in this life. I told you when you married him that if you wanted an out, we'd find a way. Here is that way."

When Janine called Maxine's psychiatric facility after breakfast, her doctor agreed to release Maxine to Janine the following afternoon. Janine could have lifted straight off the streets of Bushwick and into the smoggy skies above. Maggie joined her on the sidewalk after a bathroom break and asked, "Ready?" But all Janine could do was fling her arms around her eldest and shake with a strange mix of fear and excitement. Perhaps this would be a new era, a fresh chapter in a story that she'd thought was long over. How thrilling.

# CHAPTER THIRTEEN

## THIRTY-ONE YEARS AGO

A TWIZZLER HUNG from between Maxine Aubert's lips like a spare tentacle. Janine laughed, lifted her teeth to the other end, and then bit off a sizeable chunk.

"Don't Lady and the Tramp me," Maxine protested as the Twizzler fell between them on the bed.

"Don't waste our precious candy!" Janine countered. It was a rare thing that they scrounged up enough cash for some candy at one of their many sleepovers. They'd discovered three dollars beneath a trash can near the dollar store, stuffed it in their pockets, and then rushed away. It had been their scene of the crime and just in case, they'd purchased the candy— a bag of Twizzlers, a Three Musketeers Bar, and a classic Hershey's, at a 711 further away from Nancy and Janine's apartment, with the hope that nobody would catch wind of their treasure.

"Relaxxx..." Maxine's words had drawled out with that French accent she'd brought over the Atlantic two years before.

Janine's stomach flipped with jealousy at the sound. She knew Maxine's accent and worldly view made her "special" in school. At twelve, boys had begun to look at them differently, ogling them and pulling their hair. Maxine had power over them Janine hadn't yet mustered. This was nothing she could confess to Maxine, as she wanted to appear to know just as much as she did. How was it Maxine seemed already to own her body and her coyness like a much older, more confident teenager?

The front door of the apartment kicked open and then slammed shut. Janine froze as two sets of footsteps sauntered down the hallway and then into the kitchen. Probably, this was her mother back with whoever she ran around with just now. Lately, it had been a guy from the Bushwick Steak Shack. A few weeks ago, it had been Tyler from the local bodega. The list before that was long and varied. They never stayed for long.

Maxine gripped another Twizzler and ate the very edge of it delicately. Her own ears seemed peeled. Something was tossed onto the kitchen counter with a dramatic smash. Nancy sighed, then; it was difficult to tell if that sigh was drunken, annoyed, angry, or all three at once.

"I asked you to get me the peanut sauce?" This was Nancy, Janine's twenty-eight-year-old mother who'd long "gotten over" the idea of caring for Janine in any real way, especially since Janine had learned to cook and do her laundry around age eight.

"What?" Yep, that was the guy from the Steak Shack, back for another round of heavy, spitting arguments.

"I ask you for nothing. Just once, I want some peanut sauce. And you can't even manage."

"You're such a bitch. Do you know that? Eat your food."

The word rocketed through Janine's body. Maxine took another small bite of Twizzler as Janine curled into a ball and turned onto her side. Love for her mother was one of the only things she really knew. Sometimes, it felt as bright as the sun and just as all-encompassing. Nancy was her universe. Words spewed at her by potential lovers? They seemed like a meteor shower, threatening to destroy everything.

With Janine on her side, Maxine splayed a hand on her shoulder. "I wish they'd shut up," she said in barely a whisper.

"Me too," Janine breathed.

But the fight continued for the next twenty minutes. It evolved into what seemed like an overwrought rage before declining into what seemed to be something almost romantic, as though the two toyed with one another purposefully to get a rise out. Janine wasn't sure about the details of love. As far as she understood, between Maxine's father's divorce and the fact that Janine had never known her own father, love wasn't something you could count on. Maybe it made you babies. It certainly didn't keep your belly warm.

When Nancy and the Steak Shack guy had drunk themselves into a stupor, Maxine and Janine resumed their soft conversation. They played tapes on the tape deck and chewed on their Twizzlers and contemplated the perfect time to crack open the Three Musketeers bar, which they believed was God's gift to candy.

"Do you think we'll ever live together?" Janine whispered.

"We already practically do," Maxine pointed out. "We have sleepovers like five nights a week."

"I know, but I mean really, really live together— like we have our own place. One that doesn't change every few months, like mine. You know, where we buy only the most delicious candies and stock up and watch our favorite movies over and over again. One where we can have a cat!"

Maxine grimaced. "It sounds too good to be true, doesn't it?"

Janine's heart thudded. "What do you mean?" She clung to dreams like this as a way to map her way through time. During her darkest hours, she imagined that she and Maxine were fifteen (a seemingly impossible age) and stationed in a cozy bed somewhere in Brooklyn, dreaming sweet dreams as it snowed over a more beautiful, calmer city outside. Where was Nancy in these illusions? She wasn't sure. Her brain had to snip Nancy out if only to carve out a more beautiful world. A softer world. A world without turmoil.

"I just feel like I'm a realist," Maxine recited, using a word Janine had never heard before.

"A realist?"

"You know. I live in the real world. I know what's possible," Maxine countered. She reached for the Three Musketeers, seemingly making the decision for both of them: it was time. "Maybe we won't ever have it all. But we'll have each other. And we'll have a few Three Musketeers bars here and there. What more could we possibly need?"

Present Day

JUST PAST MIDNIGHT, Janine Grimson and Maxine Aubert piled into the guest bed at Maggie's apartment and stared into the darkness above them. Both were sober; both were scrubbed clean after separate lavender baths in Maggie's overwhelmingly large bathtub (a wedding present from Rex). Janine wanted to make a joke about what a far cry this bed was from the one they'd shared as youngsters; usually, they'd awoken covered with candy wrappers, tossing and turning against the chaos of their messiness, with smears of chocolate on their chins.

Minutes passed. Janine wondered if Maxine still didn't want to speak. She'd been very quiet and somber since Janine had picked her up and brought her back to Maggie's. Probably, she was embarrassed after her very recent trek to Maggie's. Probably, she wasn't sure what to say.

Just when Janine had committed herself to sleep, Maxine propped herself up on her elbow in the style of a much younger, much brighter girl.

"Why are you helping me?"

Janine's heart dropped into her stomach. The question hung in the air between them. If Janine closed her eyes and shifted her consciousness just so, she could almost hear Nancy growling outside to whatever deadbeat she'd brought home.

"Does there have to be an answer?" Janine breathed.

Maxine sighed. "I suppose not. It's not like closure is ever a possibility."

Janine nestled her head deeper into her pillow. Maxine seemed to stare into the dark. After another few moments of silence, Janine finally drummed up her response.

"I've been thinking a lot about everything that happened. Not just with Jack, but before about where we came from. About all we did to get to where we are. It seems impossible in many ways. And in other ways, I don't know if it was all entirely necessary. Maybe we would have been just as happy as Brooklyn waitresses. Maybe we would have been giddy and poor and living together into our twenties, swapping Three Musketeer bars and pizza slices and laughing the days away."

Maxine's voice rasped. "Things really escalated fast. I didn't know how to keep up with myself or with the money or with what money suddenly meant to me."

"It was terrifying," Janine breathed. "And I don't know why we never talked about it."

"Maybe we both wanted to pretend to ourselves, which meant we also had to pretend toward each other," Maxine murmured.

Janine leaned over to turn on the lamp. Before she could reach it, Maxine whispered, "No. Keep it dark. I want to pretend it's another time."

"You mean, you don't want to see my forty-three-year-old face?" Janine's laugh was subtle, but it didn't hold an ounce of self-pity.

"I love your forty-three-year-old face," Maxine returned. "I just like the darkness right now. It's more forgiving. If your eyes still look the way they did... I don't want to see them. Not yet."

Janine couldn't help the way she felt: still lost, still hurt, still broken. Perhaps she'd always feel a bit like that. Perhaps Maxine would always find glints of those emotions in her eyes.

After another pregnant pause, Janine whispered, "What do you think is next for us?"

Maxine blew the air out of her lips. She fell back onto her pillow and dug herself in. "That is a really good question, Jan. Only a day or two ago, I wasn't sure I'd make it to here."

Janine wanted to say she'd felt similarly over the summer when she'd learned of Maxine's betrayal. To draw them back to those old dark corners of thought, though, was criminal.

"Jack left me so much money," Janine whispered. "And I swear, I don't want it. Isn't that a weird thing to say?"

Maxine sighed. "You should keep it, honey. It's yours. He was cruel to you all those years. You should at least treat yourself to a life of luxury."

Janine shivered. "I won't be wasteful with it. I'll set myself up well. The girls, well, they'll be good forever, as will their children and their grandchildren. But I've thought so much about us, Maxine— about where we came from. The fact that we needed men to help us experience a luxurious life and other things we've done along the way. Regardless, we're beautiful, smart women."

"Cheers to that. Although, I hate it when I think about it, too," Maxine murmured. "We were and are so much more than just a rich man's wife label."

"Yes. But so are countless girls around here and across the city," Janine continued. "I think I might set up a scholarship program for girls with aspirations for themselves. I think they should come from the same neighborhood we grew up in. We could give out full-ride college scholarships, grants for art projects, and funds for start-up businesses. We could really give girls like us that boost we really needed. What do you think?"

Maxine lifted up from the pillows again, reached over, and then pulled the string on the lamp to light it, illuminating both their faces. Although Maxine remained skin-and-bone, Janine had a hunch she wouldn't be like that for long. Not around Nancy, Elsa, Carmella, and the rest of the islanders, for whom food was a necessary element, a raison d'être.

"I don't know if I ever told you this, Janine Grimson," Maxine breathed now. "But I think you're a genius."

Janine dropped her head back in laughter. Maxine tossed herself against her and hugged her as tightly as her weak frame would allow. When their hug broke, Janine beamed, slipped out of bed, and rustled through her purse. When she drew out the Three Musketeer bar, Maxine gasped with excitement.

"I haven't had one since 1997," she beamed.

"Think that was my last one, too," Janine replied as she positioned herself on the edge of the bed. "I raised the girls on fruits and vegetables for crying out loud. I don't even know if they've ever had a Twizzler."

"You really messed up as a mother," Maxine joked.

Janine tore the gooey muck of the candy bar in half and handed a portion to Maxine.

"I want to call the scholarship the Grimson Aubert Scholarship," Janine announced then.

Maxine shook her head dramatically so that her auburn hair quaked around her cheekbones. "No. You shouldn't put my name on it. I don't deserve any recognition except the word 'homewrecker.'"

"Oh, stop! You're a part of all of this, Max," Janine breathed. "It would feel wrong without you. And I want you to help me pick who gets the scholarship every year. I know, no matter how much time goes by or who we become as people, there's one thing about you that won't change."

Maxine furrowed her brow. "And what's that?"

"You love to judge people."

Maxine closed her eyes as laughter rolled over her. Slowly, she positioned her teeth over one edge of the candy bar and took a bite. The color popped into her cheeks as she felt for just a moment, the glory only twelve-year-olds across the United States truly knew.

"Oh my God, Janine," Maxine whispered as she chewed. "I've never had anything as good as this."

# CHAPTER FOURTEEN

THE SUITE at the far end of the third-floor hallway was the most sought-after room for women at the Katama Lodge. Thousand-count sheets, a claw-footed bathtub that nearly put Maggie's to shame, a hand-knitted Turkish rug that Neal had purchased on an adventure through Europe and Asia, an antique wardrobe, and a glorious bay window, with a picture-perfect view of Katama Bay just beyond. It was the perfect recipe book, a space designed for clear thoughts and clean bodies and, above all, hope. Maxine gasped at the sight and drew her arms out on either side of her, poised like a diver about to tip into the dark blue beyond.

"Is it going to work for you?" Janine asked.

Maxine rushed for the window and popped it open to allow the salty, sharp sea breeze to cascade across her cheeks. "Oh, honey. This will do just fine."

Janine had facilitated this room for Maxine's stay at the Katama Lodge and Wellness Spa. Throughout their drive back to the

Vineyard, Janine had illustrated her vision of the following weeks ahead. "I'll get you set up on a journey toward wellness and toward listening to your body and its needs. Think everything from nutrition to meditation to vitamins to yoga to acupuncture to spa treatments."

"It sounds like the most relaxing vacation of my life," Maxine had returned. "And you promise that no men will pester me while I'm there?"

"Not a man in sight," Janine had said.

Of course, Janine had forgotten that Stan Ellis remained at the Lodge in the wake of the hurricane. She and Maxine spotted him on their way down from the third-floor suite, where he hovered on the fourth rung of a ladder and straightened an old painting of the Edgartown Lighthouse.

"Stan! What are you doing up there?" Janine asked with a vibrant laugh.

"Oh, you know Nancy. I told her to put me to work, and she said not on her life. I'm making up odds and ends for me to do. Tommy ran off the island for the week and made me promise not to touch my house on my own. I guess that's what happens when you get old. Take my warning, young ladies. Use this time as you can. Hammer and nail whatever you want into any wall. This is your last chance."

Janine and Maxine burst into laughter.

"You know us too well, Stan. All we want to do is get our hands on a heavy home improvement project," Janine told him sarcastically.

"And you know how much we love wearing overalls!" Maxine offered.

Stan stepped down a rung hesitantly. Janine leaped forward and gripped the side of the ladder before it could fall back and cast Stan across the ground. They couldn't afford anything like that—not monetarily and not emotionally.

"Easy there, partner," Janine joked as she eyed Maxine, her brow heavy with worry.

"Ah, I just wanted to clamber down and go check on Nancy," Stan offered, trying to brush off the very worrying situation. "She said she'd let me cook her dinner one of these days to thank her for all her help."

Maxine's lips curved upward just the slightest bit. Janine was suddenly struck with the thought: *did Stan have a crush on Nancy?* He certainly wasn't anything like Neal, as far as Janine could tell. He wasn't "Martha's Vineyard's most beloved," as it seemed Neal had been. In fact, Stan had been the man driving the boat that had crashed years before, killing a woman who'd been beloved in the community, Anna Sheridan. That scandal had rocked the island, pushing Stan into outcast territory. He'd only recently come out of his hole, according to a few "in the know," when the Sheridan girls had returned to Martha's Vineyard to stir up trouble.

"I bet Nancy's pretty busy this evening, but there's no reason you can't ask her," Janine offered as Stan took the final rungs gently.

"With Tommy gone off across the sea again, an old man like me has to reckon with his loneliness," Stan offered, still trying to play it all off as a joke. He then saluted both Maxine and Janine, put the ladder back together again, and paraded down the hallway away from them.

"You said no men," Maxine said playfully as they continued down the staircase.

"Stan's just about as broken as the rest of us," Janine offered. "And the hurricane tearing through his house was the last straw."

"You think Nancy will ever give him a chance?"

"Nancy's a wild card, as ever," Janine explained.

"I hope I'm just as fiery at her age," Maxine said softly. "Although I hope... well..."

Janine stopped short midway down the staircase. "What do you hope?"

"I hope I find love."

Janine swallowed the lump in her throat. "That's the thing about Nancy. She found the love of her life. After all those creepy guys across Brooklyn, after all those arguments, after those guys who only paired up with her to ultimately steal from us and make us move on to the next place, Nancy still found love. I can't imagine what she thought when he died."

"If that had been me, I would have cursed the universe," Maxine offered.

"True. But instead, she reached out to me," Janine breathed.

"And you showed her how to keep going."

"We showed each other how I think. One step at a time."

---

JANINE RETURNED to the family house that evening for dinner. It had been many days since her spontaneous disappearance. The first sight of the beautiful mansion, there on its splendorous acreage at the edge of the island, shook her heart in her ribcage. Alyssa hadn't texted back much in the previous days. All Janine had been able to do in the wake of that was tell herself: *You have to trust her. She's your daughter. She's twenty-two years old. She's dealing with a barrel of grief that weighs half a ton. You never knew your father. You never knew him to hate him or love him or lose him. Have compassion— it's what you preach. So live it.*

Elsa stood upright at the kitchen counter with a blue pen poised over a calendar. When her eyes found Janine's, her smile seemed to crack open her face.

"There you are! I was worried that big bad city stole you away from us," she said. She hustled forward and wrapped Janine in a beautiful hug. "I was just making a list of everyone we want here for Thanksgiving. The Lodge is closed up that weekend, thank goodness since we all need a break. Anyone else you want to add? Henry?"

Janine's smile faltered as she perused the list. "Henry's away," she offered finally.

"Oh! Where'd he run off to?"

"He's um. He went to Portugal for a film festival and then he's off to China to film a documentary."

Her voice wavered again, betraying her. Elsa dropped her pen to the counter.

"Oh, honey. You must be sad."

"I'm not so sad," Janine countered. "It's really okay. We're just friends, anyway. We got each other through difficult times. That's all we can ask of one another."

"I don't know. What you two had..."

"It's not a big deal," Janine replied hurriedly, not wanting to get into it. She hadn't spoken to Maggie or Maxine about it at all. Her mind had been preoccupied with other things. "Anyway, is my daughter around here somewhere? I wanted to catch up with her before dinner."

Elsa's face fell toward the floor. Her cheeks looked like flat, colorless pancakes. "Are you kidding?"

Janine's heart quickened. "What?"

"I mean, I thought Alyssa went with you to New York?"

Janine felt the world tilt away from her. She crashed against the counter as she lost her footing. It was as though she'd drank too much, yet she hadn't had a drop.

"When was the last time you saw her?"

"The day you left. She was out on the beach with Cole and his friends. Then you texted you were headed to the city. I just assumed..."

"Jesus."

Janine could have lost her mind. She paced in the kitchen as Elsa scrambled to find her own phone. Panic forced her to accidentally call Bruce first. "I'm sorry. I meant to call Cole. I'll— I'll call you later." She hung up and redialed Cole, who picked up on the third ring. Janine watched her with rapt attention.

"Hey, honey. I wanted to ask you about Alyssa. She's been hanging around your friends quite a bit, hasn't she?"

Silence. Janine beckoned for Elsa to turn on the speakerphone. She couldn't take the urgency of all of this. Elsa scrambled and pressed the button to allow Cole's deep baritone to project from the speaker.

"...heard she was with Luuk, I guess, as usual. I've never seen him so captivated with someone."

Janine's heart fluttered. "Isn't this the guy who isn't even here legally?" she cried out toward the phone.

"Mom, did you put me on speaker?"

"Just answer her," Elsa blared.

"Um, yeah. He's not technically here legally, per se. But he does his job and he's good at it and I mean, what else can you say?"

Janine could have strangled her step-nephew.

"Well, what we can say is, we haven't known Alyssa's whereabouts in, what, two..."

"Three," Janine corrected Elsa.

"Three days," Elsa continued.

"Okay...well—" Cole considered this. "I can head over to Luuk's apartment and check it out."

"Would you?" Elsa asked. "Please. Stop what you're doing and go there right now. And then come home, okay, Cole? I need to see you."

Janine recognized the urgency of a mother who'd suddenly faced what it might feel like to lose someone she loved so dearly.

Cole called back twenty-five minutes later to report that Luuk wasn't at any of his regular hang-out spots and that none of his other friends had seen him since the bonfire, either. Janine's heart felt on the verge of explosion. Every time she closed her eyes, she pictured Alyssa's perfect, porcelain, sweet face as it peered up at her, asking for another story. "Just one more story, Mom."

"Maggie, hi." She had her eldest on the phone now.

"Hey! Did you two make it back okay?"

"Of course. Yes. Yes."

"You okay? You sound...panicked."

"Have you talked to Alyssa today?"

"Not since yesterday," Maggie replied. "Why? Is there a problem?"

"We don't really know where she is. She hasn't been at the house the past few days. Everyone thought she came to the city with me."

Maggie was silent. Rex's voice rang out in the background, curious about why Maggie looked so pale.

"Let me try to call her. Maybe she's screening your calls," Maggie offered.

Janine paced back and forth while Elsa poured them glasses of wine. "I just don't know what else to do with myself," she stated as Carmella entered the house. They quickly filled her in on what was happening, and Carmella suggested they call the police.

"I mean, she's twenty-two," Janine articulated. "I don't know what the cops could possibly do."

But already, Elsa had the phone to her ear and had the secretary at the police station on the line in two seconds flat. As an island girl with a good deal of credibility across Edgartown and Oak Bluffs, people paid attention to what Elsa wanted.

"I understand she's an adult," Elsa blared to whichever cop she'd nabbed at the station. "But we're worried, and we need you to look into it, Bob. I mean, your daughter's what. Twenty-one now? Twenty-two? Imagine if she'd gone missing for three days."

Around then, Maggie returned Janine's call, saying that Alyssa's phone went straight to voicemail. Her own voice shook as she said it. "I don't know what to do. I feel so lost. I wish she would have told me she was..."

"I think she's just looking for something," Janine breathed. "In all the heartache and chaos that has gone on since your father's funeral."

Elsa announced that a cop would swing by in a few minutes to interview them about potential leads. A small part of Janine's mind made up an idea of what would happen if Jack Potter himself had been there, hearing this news. "I want an FBI agent on every corner of America," he might have demanded. "I don't want a single police officer to sleep until you find her."

She wasn't a bully; she wouldn't use such words. Still, a small part of her wanted to.

Without knowing why, Janine called Maxine about an hour after she'd learned about Alyssa.

"Hi! I'm in a bath," Maxine breathed. "Just about as relaxed as I've ever felt."

Janine wanted to appreciate this moment for Maxine, but she didn't have it in her. "I'm sorry. I'm so sorry to say this, but Alyssa's gone. I'm so worried she's run off with this guy and done something stupid and I..."

"Shhh. Shhh." Maxine tried her best to steady her. "It's going to be okay. Alyssa has a good head on her shoulders. She's twenty-two years old."

Janine's knees buckled beneath her as she collapsed on the love chair in the living room. Tears coated her cheeks like paint. "I know. I know. But the last time I looked into her eyes..."

"This really hurt her. Her father."

"She hated him. But she loved him. You know the old drill."

Maxine buzzed her lips. "Do you want me to come there?"

"No. I just wanted to hear your voice. But you should keep um. Keep soaking in that bath. Doctor's orders. Okay?"

"I'll be over there as soon as I can hire someone to drive me," Maxine returned. "And get you to tell me the address."

"I'll call you in the morning when we know more," Janine countered. "Please. Just. Sit. Breathe. You've been through enough this week."

The police arrived after that. They took as much information as they could, which wasn't a whole lot, then dialed up the Oak Bluffs' ferry department, who said they'd seen Luuk head off on a ferry the morning after the bonfire.

"Was he with anyone?" Janine blared toward the cop's walkie-talkie.

"Maybe get them to go over the tape from that morning," the cop offered.

They waited in stunned silence. Elsa drank back an entire glass of wine in four minutes. Nancy arrived as the Oak Bluffs' ferry department seemed to take forever to peruse a single moment on film.

"What's going on?" Nancy demanded as her eyes like glowing orbs.

"He was with a girl," the speaker on the walkie-talkie blared now.

Janine's heart sank. She turned to face her mother, who opened her arms instinctively and took Janine in her embrace. Janine's body quivered with sobs. There was no way to know where in the hell Alyssa Potter had run off to after that. As a Potter girl, she had nothing but money; if Luuk had caught even a whiff of that, he could take advantage of her in so many different ways.

The cops left after that. Janine studied her reflection against the window that looked out over the water as Elsa, Nancy, Carmella and Mallory spoke behind her. Exhaustion permeated through every cell of her body, so much so that she wasn't sure what they said.

"She's a smart girl," Mallory offered once. "She wouldn't get herself involved in anything horrible."

Maggie called again and burst into tears. "Rex thinks I'm overreacting," she said. "But I don't know what to do with myself. She's my baby sister, you know?"

Janine heard herself walk Maggie down from the proverbial ledge. She was, first and foremost, a mother, and one of her babies needed her just then. Alyssa maybe needed her; maybe she didn't. Maybe she would think all of this pomp and circumstance was for nothing. "I can't believe you called the cops!" was something she might say later, at Thanksgiving, even, to tease them.

Maybe it would all turn into a hilarious story. Janine prayed it would. But she wasn't sure she had any prayers left.

# CHAPTER FIFTEEN

"IT'S ALL OURS, BABY," were Jack's words as he'd led Janine onto the private plane for the first time. She, age eighteen, wearing that same simple second-hand Chanel dress again, marching down the aisle between four luxurious seats, all of which faced inward to create a little circle. Janine had never even been on a plane before Jack's private plane. She had turned to him, touting a brand of arrogance she hadn't known she'd had, and said, "So, is there champagne for the flight?"

At three in the morning, Janine received a very strange call.

"Mrs. Potter." Nobody at the funeral had even attempted to call her that, thankfully. The words sent shivers down her spine.

"Hello, this is Janine speaking."

"Mrs. Potter, this is Larry."

Janine's stomach performed a strange flip. Larry. She'd known a Larry in another life.

"Hi." She furrowed her brow. "What time is it?"

"Mrs. Potter, I'm in Madrid, Spain. I have some unfortunate news."

Larry. Larry was Jack's private pilot. Larry was the man who'd flown them on their most recent, and very last, couple's trip to Hawaii. Larry had a uni-brow that crawled from one edge of his forehead to the other with a mind of its own.

Why was Larry calling her at three in the morning?

"Larry, what's going on?"

Madrid? She hadn't been to Madrid in almost fifteen years. It had been overly hot. She'd drank a strawberry smoothie in the sun and forgotten to say "gracias" when the man had taken it away. She'd cursed herself for that.

"Your daughter, Alyssa, arrived at our airport yesterday," Larry continued.

Janine snapped bolt-upright in bed. Her heart jumped into her throat.

"Bad news" now sounded much, much worse than it had before. Bad news now sounded like the worst possible news.

"She's been missing," Janine blared.

"I see." Larry seemed unwilling to give anything away too soon.

"She had a friend with her. A guy from Europe," Larry continued. "Funny accent."

Luuk.

"She offered me a boatload of cash to fly her and this guy to Madrid," Larry continued. "As you know, I just lost my main client... But still happen to have his plane. It didn't seem a far stretch for me to fly that main client's daughter over the Atlantic when she explained she had your approval. You know, Jack was nothing but good to me over the years."

"Larry. Is she okay? Or isn't she okay?" Janine's voice blared out across the Atlantic. Probably, every home between hers and Iceland and England and France and Spain itself could hear the shriek behind her words. "Larry? Tell me she's okay?"

"She's okay, Jesus," Larry returned, perplexed. "I just wanted to let you know what happened."

"Jesus Christ, Larry. All I've been doing is going insane over here," Janine cried.

"I get it. I get it. Janine, I get it." Finally, he used her real name.

This allowed Janine a soft moment of peace. She inhaled slowly and turned on the light. Now that Larry had said her daughter was safe, that she was alive, maybe she could proceed.

"This guy— this Dutch guy. And Alyssa came to you and offered you money to fly them to Madrid and assured you I said it was okay. And the plane landed safely. And everyone is in Madrid, right as rain," Janine continued. She felt as though she spoke in a stuttered morse code.

According to Larry, things started off sketchy, almost right from the get-go. But Larry hadn't received his paycheck due to legal issues in the wake of Jack's death, and he itched for a bit of cash. He agreed to the flight— but knew to keep an eye on that Luuk character.

"He was bad news," he told Janine.

Janine cursed herself, then. She'd known the man was no one to trust; she'd been able to smell it on him when he'd been directly in front of her at the beach. How had she allowed it to go this far?

"They'd obviously been out all night, partying across New York," Larry continued. "Their eyes were bloodshot. I don't know what they were on, what they'd done. Alyssa conked out during the first hour of flight while Luuk, this damn kid, kept pestering me to let him fly the plane. I told him to calm down. Grab a beer. I've never had a guy act so cavalier around flight like that, especially one who'd never driven before."

Janine tried to focus on her breathing. What time was it in Madrid? Six hours ahead? That meant it was nine in the morning.

"Anyway, Alyssa woke up again and the two of them started drinking. I don't mean normal drinking. I mean heavy. Heavy-heavy, like they have no tomorrow to look forward to," Larry continued. "I wasn't back there with them, but my stewardess, she kept popping in and out of the cockpit to tell me she wasn't sure what to do. We were only a few hours into the flight, and the two of them were belligerent. At one point, Luuk got sick into his suitcase and…"

Janine closed her eyes tightly.

"You have to know that we did everything in our power to keep him away from her after it happened," Larry continued.

"After what happened?" Janine demanded. "Larry? What the hell happened?"

"She made him mad somehow. He misheard or thought she belittled him in some way. You know these hot-headed alcoholic types. Anyway, he lunged for her, grabbed ahold of her around the neck for a second until my stewardess whacked him hard with a bottle of whiskey and knocked him out cold."

Janine didn't remember standing. She now hovered next to the bed, more awake than she'd been since childbirth.

"Janine? Are you still there?"

Apparently, Janine had let Larry the pilot rattle on and on for ages without interjecting. All she could think of was her beautiful Alyssa, terrified somewhere over the Atlantic.

"I'm here. I'm here. Larry, thank you. Thank you to you and your stewardess for saving my girl," Janine whispered.

"They've got him locked up here in Madrid waiting for an interview," Larry continued proudly. "It isn't such a good thing to attack anyone ever, but when you do it in the air on a plane, you've got a whole other thing coming."

Janine wasn't in the mood to joke. "He's from Europe, correct? Hopefully, they hold him and won't allow him to leave or come back to the USA."

"He'll be charged here in Spain, I think," Larry added. "He won't see American soil again in his life."

"And Alyssa? Can I speak with her?"

"She checked herself into The Westin Palace in central Madrid," Larry continued. "I imagine she's still sleeping off the whole ordeal. Not something I would recover from quickly, I can tell you that."

Janine thanked Larry over and over again until the meaning of the words seemed lost. She told Larry she'd be in Madrid shortly; he explained he'd have to stick around as a sort of initial witness to ensure Luuk was taken care of.

Afterward, Janine took a deep breath and looked up the phone number of The Westin Palace. Initially, when the woman at the front desk wouldn't put Janine through to Alyssa's suite, Janine put on her best Jack Potter-esque voice and said, "I believe the second name on the credit card is my own. Janine Potter." She then hunted through her wallet until she found the list of credit card numbers and read them back to the woman, who finally grunted and sent the phone call through.

A very groggy voice answered on the fourth ring. The wait for that voice was akin to torture.

"Larry?"

Of course. Larry was the only person on the planet who knew where Alyssa was.

"It's me. It's Mom."

There was silence. Janine knew better than to beg or plead to be listened to. She knew better than to press her luck. Alyssa knew what she'd done was horrendous; she knew she had run away from her feelings and ultimately into the belly of the beast. She'd been through enough.

Finally, a wail erupted from her beautiful daughter's lips.

"Mom. Mom, I wouldn't have done any of this if I'd known..."

Janine's responses were soft but also firm. "I know, honey, but what on God's green earth were you thinking? I'm just so glad you're safe and in one piece."

There was only so much you could say to someone you loved when they were so many thousand miles away.

"I'll be in Madrid as soon as I can," Janine continued. "Until then, I want you to just relax in the hotel. And no drinking. Got it?"

Alyssa chuckled good-naturedly. "Yes, I got it, Mom. I want to sleep till you get here, to be honest with you."

"As long as you don't get in any trouble," Janine affirmed. "I'll allow it."

When Janine finally got off the phone, it was four-thirty in the morning and only a week before Thanksgiving Day. Janine's bed felt like a black hole. She tip-toed out into the hallway, feeling like a child, until she found herself at Nancy's door, hovering with her knuckles against the wood. She dared herself to knock but resisted. What could she possibly say?

"I can see your shadow." Nancy's voice rang through from the other side of the door. It sounded soft and groggy. "Come in here."

The door creaked as Janine pushed it open. Nancy's doe-shaped eyes caught the soft light of the hallway.

"Were you asleep?" Janine whispered.

"No. I couldn't. Not after all that."

Janine clipped the door closed and clambered onto the edge of her mother's bed. Years before, when she had tried to do precisely this, her mother had demanded she return to her bed. "We need boundaries," she'd said to a seven-year-old, Janine.

"She's okay," Janine whispered, before bursting into tears as relief wrapped itself around her, wave after wave of it crashing over her shoulders.

In a moment, Nancy wrapped her arms around her daughter and held her tightly against her. She rocked her back and forth softly, tenderly, until Janine's sobs quieted. When they did, Nancy asked what exactly had gone wrong. Janine struggled through the story before gasping for air during the particularly rough parts.

"I don't understand it," Janine whispered as she dropped her chin to her knees and wrapped herself tighter in a ball. "The women in my life are the smartest, the most beautiful and the most stellar creatures I know, but so many of us involve ourselves with these men who manipulate us and abuse us. Why do we do it? I keep asking myself, did Alyssa watch the way Jack treated me throughout all those years and think that that's what true love is?

Will she allow this to happen over and over again? Am I not seeing something about Rex that I should be? I..."

Nancy's brow furrowed. "I've asked myself similar questions, remembering the many men I brought back to our home, Janine. How cruel they were. How much I allowed them to get away with." She shook her head as a tear ran down her cheek. "And who knows what happened before that. What did I see as a child that orchestrated my opinion of men? Is there any way out of this, truly? Carmella had, in my opinion, the world's best father and he even managed to mess her up."

Janine closed her eyes tightly as another sob escaped her lips. "I just want a single day of rest from all of this," she finally said, adding an ironic laugh. "I want to lie on the couch and watch a bad television show. I want to not think about Jack Potter for four seconds. I want to feel... like myself."

"That's the thing about it, isn't it?" Nancy whispered. "Maybe we never really feel like ourselves. Maybe we're always chasing some illusion of a past we can never return to."

Janine buzzed her lips. "Heavy, Mom."

Nancy shrugged. "Maybe I've worked in wellness for too long. The only thing I really and truly know right now is this. You need to sleep. I have a hunch you'll be on the first flight out of here, headed to Spain tomorrow. Your baby needs you."

Janine slipped between the sheets of Nancy's bed and conked out cold for nearly six hours. After she woke, she headed downstairs, where Nancy, Elsa, Carmella, and Mallory sat at the breakfast table, their faces showing the relief they all felt.

"I bought your ticket to Madrid, honey," Nancy confirmed. "Get ready. We're headed to the airport in two hours' time."

"I'll miss the Lodge," Janine told them softly, surprised that she could even use her voice after the night she'd had.

"The Lodge will miss you, too," Carmella said. "But it's withstood a whole lot before you. It just lived through a hurricane, for goodness sake. It'll stick it out without you and wait for your return. We'll get back to our routine."

"But you'd better bring her home for Thanksgiving," Elsa said pointedly as she pressed her pen against the already-prepped Thanksgiving grocery shopping list. "We've got ourselves a feast planned. Alyssa can't miss it. Not for the world."

# CHAPTER SIXTEEN

ALYSSA GAVE JANINE AN ENORMOUS GIFT: she took it upon herself to call her very worried older sister, who was furious at first but allowed her to explain the predicament point-blank. By the time Janine reached her layover at JFK to prepare for her long haul to Madrid, Maggie had booked a first-class seat for herself on the very same flight. A more enraged little creature Janine had never seen. She wore fashion-forward sweatpants, a pair of sunglasses, and a zip-up hoodie that straddled over her belly button as she made her way over to where Janine sat, sipping a nervous glass of wine. When she spoke of Alyssa, she said only, "That girl," then took a not-so-subtle bite of her bagel and grumbled inward. Janine had never been more pleased to see someone. The rest of her nuclear family cared deeply for one another and patiently waited for all of them to return. That was about as real as it got.

"I just really wonder what she was thinking? When she decided to dip into her bank account to pay Larry the pilot to take her and some Dutch guy to Madrid? I mean, I've seen Alyssa be careless before, but this careless? It's outlandish. It's…"

"She really learned her lesson, though," Janine told her. "You have to give her that."

Once on the plane, Janine and Maggie stretched themselves out on first-class seats and settled in for a seven-hour flight, complete with ever-constant wine, delectable snacks, and food with at least a hint of flavor, which, up in the air, was enough to get you through. Janine hadn't flown on a proper plane in many years, as Jack had always arranged for them to head out with Larry. Although yes, there was something incredibly bizarre about ripping into the sky over New York City with hundreds of other people, it was also oddly magical, a reminder that for some reason, all their paths had crossed as they'd all made the collective decision to head to Madrid of all places.

"What should we say to her when we see her?" Maggie asked as the plane settled itself to cruise, flattening itself out.

"I think we need to tell her how much we love her and that we're glad she's safe. She needs to know she's not alone, that we know she's going through a lot of pain and that we love her," Janine finished, then leaned back against the headrest.

Maggie's nostrils flared. "I guess I'll just tell her how much I love her, but I'm also going to kill her for panicking us the way she did. What do you think?"

"Yes, I think that's exactly what she needs to hear from you."

The flight seemed to take an eternity. Four hours in, Janine glanced toward Maggie, who had a *Vogue* magazine splayed across her stomach and her head tilted back. Her eyes were closed as she muttered to herself from somewhere in her dream world. Janine stepped lightly around her daughter and stood in the aisle for a moment. There was an eerie quality of rising up on the plane when so many of the other passengers were fast asleep. It was a silent ship, throttling through time and space, and nobody was conscious about it. Nobody seemed to care about this incredible miracle. It was too easy, these days, to forget.

Janine wandered up to the bathroom, where an older woman with dark, curly hair waited for the next available closet-sized space in the sky. The woman nodded toward the sleeping Maggie just beyond.

"Your daughter looks just like you," she whispered.

Janine blushed, grateful suddenly, that this woman had wanted to go out of her way just to link the two of them together.

"I have another one who looks a lot like me, too," Janine said. "I feel a bit spoiled about it."

"Better than the other way around. When my daughter was born as the spitting image of her father... I wanted to have a real hard talk with God about that." She wheezed slightly as she laughed, trying to keep quiet. "What do you two plan to do in Madrid?"

Janine's stomach tensed. "We're going to visit her sister, actually."

"Oh, darling. That's so fantastic. You'll have both of them close. You should do something spectacular. Something you'll never forget."

Janine laughed outright. "And what could that be?"

The woman's eyes grew shadowed. "My daughter and I always talked about taking our car across the country together and making small stops to little cafes along the way, speaking with whoever we met. We talked about creating a little travel journal, with each of us writing our thoughts and opinions about the day. We thought maybe our children or grandchildren or great-grandchildren would find it one day and learn something about us, about what we felt like or how we thought." She shrugged lightly, as though the idea was nothing she actually considered any longer.

"It sounds incredible," Janine breathed. "Why didn't it ever happen?"

The woman drew a scraggly curl behind her ear. Her eyes seemed distant, as though she now regretted the discussion. "You know. Things change. My daughter and I, well, we don't really see eye-to-eye these days. So, she doesn't want to have children. That's okay. It should have been okay. I shouldn't have said what I said..."

The woman trailed off as her eyes turned toward the ground. Janine's heart felt squeezed. How could she possibly translate all she'd learned in the previous months to this woman? That there was no end to the amount of forgiveness you could bring to the world; that if the love between her and her daughter had ever been a powerful force, there was no reason they couldn't make their way back to one another.

"Tell her how you feel," Janine whispered, her voice rasping with intensity. "She'll understand. She will."

The woman's eyes were like glass orbs. She nodded firmly as another woman exited the bathroom. It seemed she couldn't muster the strength to thank Janine, not now. But as Janine hovered in the hallway outside alone, crossing and uncrossing her arms against the chilly air of the plane, she prayed for a future in which this stranger and her daughter came together on that very road trip and cast out all doubts from the past.

THE PLANE LANDED in the capital city of Spain at eight o'clock in the morning, Spain time, which made it two o'clock in the morning east coast time. The abrasive light of the Spanish morning cut through the floor-to-ceiling windows of the immaculate airport, one that had absolutely nothing to do with the grit of JFK airport. As Maggie and Janine stepped into the halls to seek the baggage pick-up area, they were met with a flurry of sights and sounds, of multiple languages spit out from all directions, of a far different world with countless possibilities.

"You were just in Southeast Asia," Janine said to Maggie. "But to me, it feels like I haven't been away in ages. I forgot what it feels like to step out of the norm for a while. It's freeing."

Janine hailed a taxi outside as Maggie adjusted herself over their two suitcases, zipping up her sweatshirt with a flippant motion, then lifting her eyes toward the Madrid sun. With her phone back in operation, she texted Rex, only to receive an immediate call in return.

"Babe, what are you doing up?" Her voice was warm, inviting. It would suit motherhood later on when children needed something to latch onto.

"Yes, we made it. Mom's just grabbing us a cab."

The taxi driver slipped their suitcases into the car and beckoned for them to enter the backseat. Janine hopped in as Maggie closed up her conversation.

"I'll have her head on a platter within the hour," she continued. "But yes, of course. I'll tell her you love her and you're glad she's safe." The driver shut the door as Maggie added, "I love you, Rex.

Thank you for calling. And thank you for everything. I know I was a lot this weekend."

Maggie laughed as she hung up the phone and dropped her head back against the headrest. Her eyes flashed toward Janine as her cheeks burned red with embarrassment.

"I cried a lot," Maggie whispered. "About Alyssa. About Maxine. About Dad. I was an emotional rollercoaster. Rex didn't know what to do. He canceled all his plans and just stayed in with me, holding me till I fell asleep. He even ordered my favorite Chinese food."

As the driver swept them into the bustling city streets of Madrid, Janine feasted her eyes on as much of the city as she could make out: the old-world Romanesque architecture, the bright yellows, oranges and reds of the painted buildings, the beautiful people on the streets who used their hands to speak vibrantly as the Spanish cut through the air.

"At least I get to kill Alyssa in such a beautiful place," Maggie remarked with a smirk. "It could be a drag otherwise."

They arrived at the Westin and stepped out onto the sidewalk as a bell boy bustled forward to retrieve their bags. Janine had booked a suite for the three of them to stay in together while they decided what to do next. A Spanish concierge stepped into the foyer upon their entrance to greet them, explaining that Jack Potter had been a frequent guest at the hotel and he was *"terribly sorry for your loss."* Janine was so surprised to hear those words again, after so much heartache, that she hardly reacted.

The concierge informed them that Alyssa had moved to the new suite that morning. "Our staff assisted her in the move. She's resting comfortably on the terrace, waiting for you."

Janine and Maggie stepped into the elevator and pressed the button to the highest floor. Throughout their ride, they didn't dare speak. The entire journey felt surreal and outside of time. When the elevator pinged, they rushed down the hallway and made their way into the suite, which was blustery and fresh with a morning breeze.

Alyssa stepped out from the terrace. She wore a maroon dress, which was tight around the bodice and then fluttered out over her legs. Her eyes were far away and sunken in, as though she'd spent the previous few days crying.

Words weren't necessary. Maybe they never really were.

Janine and Maggie rushed toward the final piece of their family puzzle. They wrapped their arms around her and held her firmly as the first of probably many cries erupted from Alyssa's throat. She shook against them as she wept. Janine closed her eyes and tried to shove away all thoughts of, *"What if she hadn't been safe? What if everything had gone wrong? What if? What if?"* As a parent, you couldn't always live in the what-if. Sometimes, you just had to live in the now.

They sat around the breakfast table on the terrace as a full feast arrived for them: fresh bread and olives and cheeses and pastries, buckets of piping-hot coffee and even mimosas and bright tart strawberries.

"I haven't left the hotel much," Alyssa said after a while. "The police came here to interview me, which was kind of them. I've been doing laps in the swimming pool as a way to get my mind off of things." She gave the slightest shrug as she turned her eyes back to the food between them.

Silence fell once again. Alyssa took a long sip of the bubbling juice, then whispered, "I don't know what I was thinking."

Janine's heart dropped into her stomach. "The last thing I want you to do is beat yourself up about this."

"I was reckless," Alyssa breathed. "I was reckless about everything. You wanted to bring me back to the Vineyard so that we could be together, hold each other up after Dad's..." She trailed off as though the word "death" remained too powerful. "But I just hated the fact that Dad being gone meant that I had to think about him all the time. It seemed so entirely like him since he was so obsessed with himself. Suddenly, I just wanted to forget— about New York, about that apartment we grew up in, and about Dad and his stupid arrogance. Especially the way he'd died like that, too young, before I could fully understand him."

Janine's face was marred with sorrow and sadness. She could feel the pain within her daughter and wanted to make it disappear.

"When I met those guys, Cole's friends, I suddenly saw an opportunity to forget," Alyssa breathed. "I wanted to pretend to be an island girl. A girl that didn't have to do anything or worry about anything— as long as there was enough beer to go around. And then one day, when I'd tossed back a few too many, I made it up in my mind that I'd fallen in love with that guy."

Maggie drew her hand over Alyssa's on the table.

"We've all fallen for the wrong guy," Maggie whispered. "It's not a reason to hate yourself. Men can say beautiful things. They can be beautiful liars. It's not up to us to think that every person we meet is a liar, necessarily."

"But I should have known that my guard was down," Alyssa whispered. "And I shouldn't have dipped into my money like that. I know that we come from a unique position. I know that most people— people like you, Mom... that you weren't born with such privilege. I suddenly couldn't understand my privilege. I just wanted to be free. And I wanted to use Dad's stupid money to get me as far away as I could."

Maggie rushed up and drew her arms around Alyssa as another sob escaped. This was the real Maggie: the ultimate comforter, the shoulder to cry on. For all her threats, she was about as soft as they came.

"I just can't believe I fell for someone just as toxic as Dad," Alyssa cried then as tears rushed down her cheeks. "I can't believe I found myself in a position where... where... I actually thought he was going to..."

The fear that beamed off of Alyssa's face was enough to break Janine's heart. She gathered herself around both Maggie and Alyssa and curled against them, like a mother hen over her newborn chicks. Her girls swam with a million thoughts, fears, feelings and stories; more would follow them through time. How lucky she was to have them. How lucky she was, even now, to receive the honest story from Alyssa. Hearing someone's honesty was a unique privilege. Janine didn't want to squander it. Ever.

That afternoon, Janine, Maggie, and Alyssa collapsed in separate king-sized beds for two-hour naps. Afterward, Janine convinced her girls to head out on the town for dinner and drinks. En route to the restaurant, they stumbled into a number of boutique shops, all of which had her fashion-obsessed daughters salivating.

"I just want to try on one more thing," Alyssa called to her mother, who hovered near the door with her bags of new silk scarves, a skirt, and a bracelet.

Alyssa wanting to try on one more thing at the store was a normal thing. Maybe this was how things went: inch-by-inch, you returned to stasis. Inch-by-inch, you relearned how to breathe.

Outside, Janine lifted her phone from her purse. To her surprise, she had a message from Henry. They'd been so quiet; it had felt like a cease-fire.

The message held a single, crooked selfie, in which Henry grinned sheepishly and held up a gold-plated award.

**HENRY: Can you believe these guys? I barely even got into the festival and then they up and decided I deserved an award.**

**HENRY: I hope this humble-brag isn't too annoying.**

**HENRY: I hope you're doing well, Janine.**

**HENRY: And I hope it's okay that I reach out from time to time.**

**HENRY: You really made the past six months special for me. I don't know what I would have done without you.**

"Mom?" The voice seemed to ring out from another world as Janine read and reread Henry's messages. "Mom, hello? You there?"

Janine lifted her eyes to find Maggie before her, her brow furrowed with worry.

"I'm here," Janine breathed. "And, if you girls are willing, I might have an idea for an adventure."

# CHAPTER SEVENTEEN

"I JUST THOUGHT it would be more romantic if we did it Thelma and Louise style," Alyssa recited as she flung the three-dimensional paper map across her thighs and swept her finger across it, hunting for the appropriate highways. Janine was in the driver's seat of the rented vehicle, her fingers bright white as she tried to maneuver Spanish traffic out of the city. It was frantic and harried; horns blared from all directions. "Terrified" was linked to "feeling alive."

"Alyssa? I think it's very sweet you want to use a physical map. I really do. But by the time you figure out which exit I should take, I think we might wind up in a huge pile-up," Janine said, trying to keep her tone even. "Use that piece of technology you normally have glued to your hand and get the directions up."

But Maggie, who was sitting in the back seat, already had them ready. "You're going to want to take this next exit, Mom. It sweeps right up here—"

Just in the nick of time, Janine drove the vehicle from the side street out onto the highway. This allowed them to leave Madrid and drive across the rest of the great country of Spain and then into Portugal, where the man she thought she could be in love with would remain for a few days more before his big trek to China.

Janine had described the situation to her daughters over dinner the previous evening. As the cocktails had rolled over her, her speech had grown more frantic. "I've never loved anyone except your father," she'd explained, perhaps too pointedly. "And maybe I never thought I deserved anyone who treated me kindly. I felt like this push-pull of having someone who loved you enough to be possessive and cruel to you was what 'love' really was. I've been wrong about so many things in my life. And I regret so much if I instilled any of those values in you two."

Maggie had admitted she'd had a handful of relationships with that dynamic before finding Rex, who was "as sweet as can be." Alyssa had just shrugged and said, "Not sure if you know what just happened to me, but I think it's possible I just have crappy luck when it comes to romance and men in general." She'd then continued to say, "But if you and Henry have something—something real, then it's proof we can all work through our horrible attachment issues and heal. And dammit, that's something I want to work for. Let's drive to him tomorrow before he goes."

Now that Janine had both her girls in the car with her, she was reminded of that woman on the plane, the woman who now dreamed about a potential road trip with her daughter, one that dug deep into all the things they'd always wanted to say but never had. How close could you ever truly be to the people you loved the most? Was it ever possible to really know them? Janine wanted to fight to figure that out.

The drive from Madrid to Lisbon was approximately six hours, with several breaks in-between for bathrooms and snacks. She and the girls made it their mission to taste-test several of the Spanish gas station snacks, which made their stomachs ache even as their conversations zipped along with the benefit of added sugar.

"This region is beautiful," Alyssa remarked suddenly, mid-way through her five-star assessment of a Spanish snack. "The mountains, vegetation and just everything, in general, is so beautiful and different from what you see back at home. It looks like a different world set in another time."

The ragged brown mountains swept along either side of them, an ever-present reminder that they weren't on the Vineyard any longer. The ripping wild winds of the east coast were miles and miles away.

"Soak up this Spanish sun," Maggie affirmed. "We have a dark winter ahead of us."

"And I can't wait," Janine added. "Warm soups and chili with cornbread on cozy afternoons at the house with Mom. Thanksgiving is just a few days away, and Elsa said she would personally destroy each of us if we missed it."

"We wouldn't miss it for the world," Alyssa added softly. "Especially not this year after what we've all been through and with so many changes that have happened."

"Maybe this will be the beginning of a new tradition," Maggie offered. "Now that your life has changed so much over the past year... we have to celebrate that."

As they neared Lisbon, the conversation drifted toward what Janine might do when she saw Henry for the first time.

"It's really hard to say or even predict what will happen," Alyssa said as she wagged a gummy worm through the air to highlight her point. "He's definitely going to be shocked to see you and I think you should tell him how you feel. Why hold back? We only get so much time on this earth, so why waste it. Right?"

Janine and Maggie nodded in agreement, then Maggie asked, "Do you know what you're going to say?"

"I have no idea. It's not like I wrote a speech down or something." Janine replied as her heart thumped.

Maggie and Alyssa seemed to have an entire conversation through their eyes at that moment.

"Don't hold out on me! What are you thinking?" Janine demanded.

"Just speak from the heart, I guess," Maggie returned.

"You know that never works," Alyssa said.

"Henry's different. He's very soft-hearted and he has a lot of compassion," Maggie stated as though she knew him better than most people. Her words made Janine smile from ear to ear.

"Yeah. I can picture him as a 'having long walks on the beach and holding your hand' type of guy," Alyssa affirmed.

"I don't know where you girls come up with this stuff," Janine said. "You've dated much, much more than me. Once upon a time, I was a waitress. And then boom, I met a handsome billionaire... and now, I'm here."

"Your story is so much crazier than either of ours, but we can't compare," Alyssa countered. "You should really write a book. A tell-all."

"No," Janine said firmly. "I've had enough press over the past few years for a lifetime. All those times, I had to make sure what I wore to the grocery store was perfect, just in case a photographer took a photo of me and sold it to the tabloid papers. I remember once they posted one of me in a sweatshirt with the caption, 'Billionaire Jack Potter's wife steps out in massive sweatshirt, hiding potential weight gain. Pregnant?'"

"Oh my gosh, I know. They're shameless about stuff like that," Maggie remarked.

Janine pulled over about an hour outside of Lisbon to grab a bottle of water and take a deep breath. In the gas station, she spotted a little notebook on sale for one euro and purchased it along with a blue pen. When she returned to the car, she explained to her daughters what the woman on the plane had said about recording what they thought and how they thought it, about leaving a record behind for loved ones in the future.

"We've lost something in this modern age," Janine told them both. "We're just a collection of text messages and social media updates. How will anyone understand who we are? What will be left? When I came to Martha's Vineyard to try to get to know your grandmother, I would have been really lost had I not discovered a collection of photographs and old letters she'd saved. They were proof that she still cared, that she loved me."

Alyssa and Maggie both agreed to write several lines in the notebook about their father's death, about the trip to Spain, about Maggie's new marriage to Rex, and about their dreams for what came next.

Janine parked the car a quarter-mile from the Lisbon Film Festival. Too frightened, suddenly, to leave the vehicle, she lifted her pen to the notebook to scribe her thoughts. Her pen quivered above the lines.

"I think you should talk to Henry first before you make any assumptions about what comes next," Alyssa interjected then.

Maggie reached up from the backseat to try to grab the pen, but Janine waved her off.

"Let me just write one thing before I go in there," Janine whispered. "One thing and then after I talk to Henry, after we do this love quest, then I'll write an entry about how terribly I failed."

"Don't talk about yourself like that, Mom. It's like the first rule of mental health. Build yourself up. Believe in yourself," Alyssa countered before she added, "I mean, that's what I'm trying to work on, myself."

"Me too," Maggie breathed from the back.

Janine nodded firmly. If her girls believed in the power of internal words, she had to, too. She then lifted her pen and wrote a single line— it was something powerful enough to build everything else upon.

*"Whatever happens next,"* she wrote, *"I will find a way through it. I will know there will be good things again. I won't expect those good things from other people— but only myself. Nobody else has power over me to alter my happiness. It comes from within."*

She showed the words to Maggie and Alyssa, who nodded formally, exchanged glances, and then said in unison: "Okay. She's ready."

Janine added another smear of lipstick before she headed into the quieter, softer Portuguese sun. She had opted for a dark green linen dress, which allowed for a particularly good view of her long, athletic legs and her slender shoulders. Maggie and Alyssa agreed to wait at a coffee shop nearby while Janine headed into the film festival itself.

According to the website, there was a second showing of Henry's well-received documentary, set to begin at four that afternoon. It was now three-thirty. Janine could only hope to fling herself into the throngs of other humans, hunting for him. It had to go right. There was no other way through.

But once in the massive theatre, Janine understood the depths of her mistake. Back on Martha's Vineyard, Henry was her own: her dearest friend, the person she could easily call at three in the afternoon to meet for a coffee at three-thirty. Here, across the Atlantic Ocean, Henry was a hot commodity, one of the finest up-and-coming documentarians, and everyone who was anyone had come out to watch the show of his newest accomplishment. Even the main hall was stuffed to the gills with filmmakers and viewers alike.

"The way he handles the ever-shifting narrative is to die for," one person complimented in a high-pitched English accent as Janine cut past, her eyes scanning everywhere for him.

When she reached the front door of the theater, a man with a scanner demanded her ticket.

"I don't have one," she explained.

"There are still seats. It's our biggest cinema," he told her.

Janine grumbled. She'd wanted to get this over and done with before the documentary rather than after. She texted her daughters that she had to stick it out until afterward. Both admitted they'd already found a number of shopping streets they wanted to hit up before their departure from Lisbon.

Janine settled into a seat toward the back-left of the cinema, nestled between a woman from Valencia, Spain and a film instructor from India, both of whom asked her about her familiarity with Henry Dawson's work. It was surreal. Janine wanted to tell them that she had spent the better part of the summer helping Henry to arrange interviews for little quasi-documentaries that involved the island on which he'd been born. In this space, it felt silly to even mention any of that.

One of the film festival organizers appeared center-stage and spoke a bit about Henry and his commitment to documentary cinema. He called him one of the most exciting visionaries of the early twenty-first century. And then, he gestured out across the crowd to point to where Henry was seated, in the very middle and down below. A blonde woman sat alongside him, leaned toward his ear, and whispered something as the crowd roared with applause. Janine's stomach churned so violently that she thought she might vomit.

The documentary was something Henry had filmed the year prior to his arrival to Martha's Vineyard, the year before his mother's death. It involved an impoverished community in West Virginia and how they'd come together to build a community center for the betterment of their children's involvement and education. Many of the people within the documentary couldn't read; many struggled to get together enough money to feed their children. The film spoke about the wage gap within the United States and just how horrific it was that people had to struggle so greatly just to eat. But it also involved joy and loyalty and deep, impenetrable love, the kind you couldn't get rid of even in the darkest of eras.

The film was incredible. When the lights came up, Janine touched her cheek to find it wet with tears. She again remembered what Jack had said all those years ago when he'd backed one of Henry's projects. "Henry is a visionary— a true artist. You just don't just stumble into those kinds of people anymore."

The applause filtered out as the film festival organizer stood once more and suggested that Henry come to join him to field questions from the audience. Janine's heart fluttered, as swift as the wings of a butterfly. He looked incredibly handsome, sun-tanned from the Portuguese sun and vibrant from its wide selection of seafood. He greeted everyone in Portuguese as though he'd recently picked up the language fluidly.

Janine's fluttering heart soon transplanted itself to a drum. She closed her eyes languidly and waited, listening as several other people in the audience thrust their hands in the air to ask their questions. After the fifth person, Janine finally lifted her hand. It quivered above her like a balloon in the air.

The festival organizer continued to evade her. He pointed at everyone else as her hand continued to shake.

But finally, for reasons unknown to her, Henry's eyes found hers in the crowd. He was mid-way through answering someone's question when he then stuttered into silence. His eyes were warm and nourishing; staring into them was like falling into the softest sleep.

"I think we have one more question. Toward the back left," Henry announced finally into his microphone after he'd finished with the others.

Janine's knees quaked as she stood. The Indian film instructor on her left-eyed her as though she was a bomb about to go off. Silence fell over the cinema.

"Hello, I'm Janine Grimson from the United States," she

introduced herself, mirroring the others. "I'm curious about your future projects. I've heard rumors about a particularly personal and sensitive documentary with a focus on your home located on Martha's Vineyard. Any chance us viewers will get a sneak peek into Henry Dawson's heart-of-hearts with that in the coming year?"

Henry's face drained of color. She prayed he understood the actual question behind her question: *will you come home? Will you be with me? Do you understand that I can't live without you?*

Henry's hand shook as he lifted his microphone.

"You seem to have insider information," he responded softly, which resulted in several of the audience members chuckling. "And to answer your question, yes. In fact, I was recently asked to help out on another's documentary in Asia— but I plan to turn down the project to ensure I can go back to my own vision. I guess I'm a little egomaniac when it comes to that— filming other people's projects? Giving over control? Other men and women are much stronger than me in that regard."

Janine's heart leaped into her throat.

"So, to answer your question, I will return rather soon to Martha's Vineyard to finalize the last scenes of that documentary. Besides that, I've heard killer things about their holiday season. With Thanksgiving right around the corner, you wouldn't catch this American anywhere else."

# CHAPTER EIGHTEEN

JANINE WAS USHERED out of the cinema, where she hovered like a lost dog as the rest of the audience streamed out on either side. Bubbling conversation in a variety of languages felt akin to a sea between herself and the man she was falling in love with. For years, she'd been the butt of every one of Jack's jokes. He'd belittled her, counted her as someone so far beneath him that her feelings weren't anything to be considered in the grand scheme of the rest of his decisions, and assumed only that if he threw money at her, at their situation, she would be content to sit around and allow the world to roll on without her. In a sense, his affair with Maxine had been the single greatest thing to happen to her in over ten years. It had kick-started her life in a sense.

Something that Henry had said during his Q&A session had been this: "It's a funny thing about documentary stories. You, as the filmmaker, have to watch them unravel before you. You can't plan for anything. It builds a world of surprises. I suppose it's a good lesson to bring with you to normal life. Most of the time, the best things are the things you could never have planned for. Things you could never have imagined."

Henry pierced through the crowd. His eyes latched onto hers as he whisked through, walking with a purpose and a certainty Janine had never seen him wear. When he reached her, she swam into his arms and allowed herself to be held, really held, just in the way he'd held her that night after she'd returned from Jack's funeral.

This time, when their hug broke, she tipped herself onto her tippy-toes and kissed him. Her belly churned with excitement and wonder and joy. His hands linked themselves together at the base of her back, uniting their torsos as they kissed longer, deeper. Maybe they'd said all the words they needed to say over the previous six months. Maybe now, their bodies had to take over.

"You were incredible today," Janine finally whispered when she came up for air. "I couldn't believe it."

Henry bowed his head. "When I saw you in the crowd, I thought you were an illusion. I've been seeing you everywhere, Janine. On street corners. In cafes. In every cinema. But this time... this time you were really you."

"I'm really me. Or, a work in progress of me, I suppose," Janine breathed.

Henry admitted he had to return to the festival organizers to discuss more proceedings. Janine said she had to get back to her daughters, that they planned to drop off the car at the Lisbon airport before taking Jack's private plane back to Martha's Vineyard.

"Elsa will have all our heads if we're not at her Thanksgiving dinner table," she explained with a wry laugh.

Henry nodded firmly. "I have to believe that. Elsa's about as sweet as they come, but get her angry..."

"She can turn on a dime."

---

JANINE FLOATED BACK to find her daughters, who perched on a bench with shopping bags lining the sidewalk around them. Alyssa flung her arms around her mother after she briefly explained what had happened. Maggie beamed, impressed.

"Mom, I'm so proud of you. You're everything that I wish to be and then some," Maggie told her with every single ounce of love in her.

Janine smiled as she felt her heart grow the size of a balloon. "Thank you, honey. That means the world to me."

They drove back out to the airport, where Larry met them with the private plane. Janine hadn't been on board in over a year but was surprised that entering it felt akin to slipping on an old glove. Many of Jack's things remained within: bottles of scotch he'd planned to drink, books he'd planned to read, and even a DVD collection of a documentary series about American presidents he had always planned to watch.

"We'll have to sell this old thing," Janine said to the girls as they buckled themselves in. "No reason on earth we should have a private plane. Your dad wanted to crawl all over the world, eating it whole. We don't need that."

"I have no interest in being anywhere but the Vineyard for the time being," Alyssa announced. "I'll look back into city life in January. But from here straight through till December 31, I plan to stuff myself with Vineyard turkeys and Christmas desserts and watch buckets of Christmas specials with you and Grandma, that is if you'll have me, of course."

As Larry started up the plane, Janine checked her messages, as she'd neglected her phone over the previous few hours. One was from Maxine, featuring a photo of her and a beautiful, nutritionally dense salad handcrafted from the beautiful kitchen at the Katama Lodge. In the photo, Maxine's skin seemed to glow.

**MAXINE: I just had my first acupuncture appointment with Carmella. Now— salad! I love the schedule you made up for me. I feel committed to myself, both mentally and physically, in a way I haven't in years, so thank you for that!**

Janine hurriedly typed back.

**JANINE: You look fantastic! The Lodge is closed up for Thanksgiving (I would imagine they told you), but we'd love to have you for Thanksgiving if you'll have us in return.**

**JANINE: See you soon.**

The other message was from the lawyer in charge of Jack's will and estate.

"Just read your letter regarding the potential scholarship program for girls in Brooklyn," he wrote. "It's a fantastic idea. Come to the city after the Thanksgiving holiday so we can discuss it more."

Janine's heart thudded with excitement. She pressed her phone to her chest as the plane surged down the runway before lunging into the bright blue sky. The world that awaited them back on

Martha's Vineyard was a chilly, grey one— but it was home and she would welcome it with open arms. She'd run off to Europe to save her daughter, a daughter she had recently learned couldn't be fully protected, not from all the evils of the world (or the evils within her own mind). In the meantime, she'd also taken a huge risk, something that could have very well altered the course of her life. She had to be brave enough for whatever came next.

# CHAPTER NINETEEN

THE HOUSE WAS a flurry of pre-Thanksgiving activity. Janine and her daughters arrived home Wednesday afternoon, which allowed them a front-row view of Elsa at her most holiday-manic. She bossed Cole from one end of the house to the other and all across Edgartown and Oak Bluffs, demanding him to pick up specialty bread and cheeses, the finest wines, and new decorations for the big meal ahead. Just after Janine entered the kitchen after their return, Janine paused to watch as Elsa ran a pen over her long list of to-dos, muttering to herself.

"You okay, sis?" Janine offered, calling Elsa a term she'd never used before.

Elsa blinked up with surprise. She dropped her pen to the side of the to-do list. "You're back!" She then took two strides toward Janine and wrapped her up in a huge hug. "Gosh, that was all so traumatic." She leaned back and slid a hand over Janine's hair. "Tell me our girl is okay. Gosh, I almost killed Cole when I heard more about this guy. The fact that he let Alyssa near him..." She trailed off as her cheeks burned red with anger.

"Let's not talk about it right now," Janine breathed. "We're moving forward. That's in the past where it belongs and needs to stay. It's time for Thanksgiving— for gratitude and feeling the love of our family. Worries can find us again when they need us."

"Beautifully said," Elsa stated with a nod of her head.

Maggie and Alyssa bustled in with their suitcases and shopping bags, hollering hellos to Elsa and Cole, who was up to his elbows in plaster, as Elsa had instructed him to hang a new shelf in the dining room. "We need it to put up the new Thanksgiving and Christmas decorations," she explained as Cole grumbled his own hellos. He soon went to the sink, scrubbed himself clean, and gave Alyssa the kind of hug only a brother would give a sister: a powerful one that meant *I'm sorry. I won't make that mistake again. And I'll protect you as long as we both shall live.*

When their hug broke, Alyssa wiped tears from her cheeks but soon flipped her mood to suit her next mission: to tell her Aunt Elsa what a badass her mother was, as she'd charged directly into Henry's film festival showing and basically demanded him to come home.

"That's not how it happened," Janine corrected as her own cheeks took on color.

"What? It's not how what happened?" Nancy appeared in the doorway, having taken a nap upstairs (one that she'd probably set up to avoid Elsa's harried approach to the holiday season).

Alyssa and Maggie hugged their grandmother and explained the fuller story of Henry, which culminated in them saying Henry would be around for Thanksgiving dinner. Elsa hurried back to her list, where she scribed, "Another chair??" toward the bottom.

Nancy scuttled toward the basement to grab a couple of bottles of wine. Very soon, everyone had a glass in hand as Elsa drew out ingredient after ingredient from both the fridge and the cabinets, explaining the Thanksgiving menu to Janine.

"Carmella should be back from the Lodge within the hour," Elsa continued. "She told me she wants to make the pies. Should I not have trusted her with that? I mean, it's a huge part of the day. Pumpkin pie, apple pie, and lemon meringue are a huge responsibility."

Janine wanted to chuckle at Elsa's fears surrounding this seemingly silly holiday of endless eating, but she knew it represented so much more to Elsa. She'd lost her husband. She'd lost her father. She'd moved out of the home she'd raised her children in so that she could get back up on her feet and push herself forward through time. Now, she'd fallen in love again; she'd found a purpose in the world. And this Thanksgiving was the representation of putting that all together. It was a thoughtful act of love.

"How can I help?" Janine finally said after Elsa finished out her fearful rant.

Very soon, Janine, Alyssa, and Maggie had a sort of three-woman assembly line going in order to make the seven-layer salad. Carmella arrived with several bags of apples and a few pumpkins, which she set to work on in the far corner of the kitchen. Nancy entered and snapped on some Michael Bublé music, saying it was 'finally time to get the holiday spirit going in there."

"No holiday spirit here, Nancy," Carmella joked. "Elsa's got us on a strict schedule. We're more like Santa's elves."

Nancy giggled and set to work on her own Thanksgiving responsibilities, as she'd agreed to make a huge pot of mashed potatoes and gravy. Elsa bustled in and out of the kitchen, tending to things and mumbling to herself about the turkey and stuffing.

"What did you girls do last year for Thanksgiving?" Nancy asked then.

It was a strange question, given the current circumstances. In nearly every sense, Janine, Nancy, Maggie, and Alyssa were about as tight as peas in a pod; in another sense, they hadn't spent any time together prior to June of that very same year.

After an awkward pause, Maggie tried her hand at an answer.

"Dad always hired an elaborate Thanksgiving chef. The food was to die for, but it was also pretty soulless. He also always invited a number of business associates. Sometimes, their kids came, which was fun for Alyssa and me because we usually disappeared to one of our bedrooms while the adults talked about the stock market or whatever."

"My, how things change," Nancy murmured now.

It was true. If Janine closed her eyes for just a moment and convinced herself it was only three-hundred and sixty-four days ago — not so long in the grand scheme of things— she could practically feel the boom of Jack's voice as he spewed arrogant and confident language over their dinner guests, both embarrassing her and making her somehow proud to be associated with such a strong and powerful man. She was nothing compared to him, especially back then. She'd given up on her holistic practices. She'd cowered to him becoming his wife and only his wife. She'd felt like a Stepford wife.

Maxine had been at the previous Thanksgiving, and the one before, and the one before. Sometimes, throughout Jack's pompous Thanksgiving speeches, Janine and Maxine had lock eyes over the table. They'd had to bite their tongues several times in order to keep from bursting into laughter like children. At the time, Janine had felt inextricably linked to this woman; she'd been her light in the darkness.

Carmella snuck each of the overly-stuffed apple and pumpkin pies in the oven. The house brewed up a beautiful, spiced aroma as Nancy dropped down along the fireplace and added several logs within. Janine, Maggie, Alyssa, and Mallory gathered around in the living room and watched as the fire engulfed the logs, casting them in a warm glow. Alyssa lay her head delicately over Janine's shoulder as her eyelids drooped.

Elsa bustled in and out of the living and kitchen area in preparation for the following day. Finally, Carmella came out of the kitchen and pushed Elsa into a comfy chair, then said, "You've done all you can do tonight. There's nothing else to prepare. Tomorrow will come regardless of how many things you worry about today."

Pizza was ordered— several enormous crispy-dough, cheese-laden pies from the Edgartown Pizza Joint, where the delivery driver knew their name (and knew they tipped well). Maggie popped open another bottle of wine and made the rounds as Nancy and Alyssa squabbled over which movie to watch for a cozy evening in. With each syllable and each laugh and each sip of wine, Janine found herself enveloped deeper in the sincere joy of having the ones she loved the most around her.

Around the time that the pizza arrived, Janine received a message from Henry.

**HENRY: Plane just landed.**

**HENRY: I'll be at your place tomorrow, fully prepared for a feast.**

**HENRY: I can't wait to see you.**

**HENRY: I've been thinking about you so much.**

Janine pressed her palm over her heart as her eyelids closed. Alyssa called her out almost immediately for "swooning." Nancy said, "Let her swoon. She certainly deserves it." At this, Alyssa wrapped her arms around her mother's waist, planted a kiss on her cheek, and told her, "You do deserve all the love in the world, Mom. You really do."

Carmella and Elsa gathered the pizzas across the overly-large antique dining room table to allow for everyone to come, grab their slices and their plates, and then return to the roaring fire of the living area. Janine watched herself put three slices of pizza on her plate, like some sort of happy version of herself, one who hadn't a care in the world about carbs or calories. Maybe that's what the secret to happiness was: not sweating the small stuff, learning to find the beauty in everything and finding a reason to smile, despite the darkness of the approaching winter and all the sorrows that had come before.

Cody arrived with his toddler, Gretchen, around eight-thirty. Gretchen was passed out across his shoulder with the slightest bit of drool dribbling across her chin. Carmella led Cody up to her room, where they had a little bed all set up for Gretchen. Already, Cody had slipped easily into their family dynamic. Gretchen was a part of the equation and Carmella welcomed that equation with warm, open arms.

Back downstairs, Cody ate a slice of pizza and listened to the adventures of Maggie, Alyssa, and Janine, sans the part with Luuk and the airplane. Those stories weren't for gathering around and gossiping.

Carmella wrapped an arm around Cody's back as he asked several questions about the food in Spain, about the architecture in Portugal. He seemed captivated.

"You know, Carm, I really think we should take a trip over there," he said excitedly. "I've always wanted to try out my high school Spanish."

"Donde estas?" Carmella teased. "Mi llamo ist..."

"Que linda," Cody returned in a lilting voice as Carmella blushed.

There was a soft pause. Janine felt the energy shift slightly, as though everyone had just taken a collective sigh and allowed themselves to relax deeper into their couch cushions. Cody made a funny noise in the back of his throat.

"Can I get you something to drink?" Carmella asked suddenly.

"No, no. I have this." Cody grabbed his wine and swung it back, taking admittedly too much in a single sip. He then grimaced and placed the wine back on the floor. "Now that I have everyone's attention, I have something to say."

Everyone was captivated. Cody shifted his weight as he turned his eyes back toward Carmella. Each time he looked at her, Janine was reminded of Henry's eyes when he'd first spotted her in the crowd at the film festival. It was a pure kind of love. It was what the world revolved around.

"I wanted to wait till tomorrow, but I just don't think I can. I won't be able to eat or drink or concentrate," Cody said softly. He then dropped to one knee before Carmella and gripped both of her hands. "Carmella, the previous few months of our romantic relationship have been the best months of my life. I've known you since I was just a kid. You've seen my darkest moments; you've been a part of my lightest moments. And I want you there through thick and thin."

There was another dramatic pause. Janine watched Carmella's face, wondering if she would ever have such a similar joy. Carmella deserved this far more than anyone she knew. She had spent decades of her life alone, feeling alienated from the rest of her family.

"I love you more than life. Will you marry me, Carmella Remington? Will you make me the happiest man in the world?"

Carmella's eyes were rimmed with tears. Slowly, she nodded before laughter erupted from her very soul and she fell forward and wrapped herself around him like a child trying to climb a tree.

"Does that mean yes?" Cody asked as laughter bubbled up around each of them.

"I think you've got yourself a fiancé, Cody," Nancy beamed. "I'll be right back. I think this calls for champagne."

# CHAPTER TWENTY

JANINE'S CHILDHOOD Thanksgiving's hadn't been particularly fruitful. Sometimes, Nancy had thrown a few things together— never turkey, but sometimes chicken, mashed potatoes and gravy, and either ice cream or pie. Janine had memories of watching the Thanksgiving Day parade from her Brooklyn television set, while other children sat along the streets just a mile or so away and watched the festivities live. It had always seemed that Thanksgiving joys were other people's joys— just something you saw on television and never in real life.

When Janine had gotten a bit older, she and Maxine had found their way to one another during the Thanksgiving holiday, which had resulted in a funny mix of cookies eaten and wine coolers drunk. As teenagers, they scrambled across the Brooklyn streets, trying and usually failing to get themselves into scrapes. Often, they'd collapsed in front of a Christmas movie around ten or eleven, watching the dim light of the television until their half-crazed ideas diminished and they were allowed the quiet of sleep.

Maxine appeared at the door of the house at eight-thirty in the morning, a surprisingly early time for a woman who'd assuredly lived a life of leisure the previous twenty or so years. She wore simple jeans, high heels and a turtleneck, a far cry from the outfits she'd normally worn back in Manhattan, and her makeup was simple, her hair straight. She gathered Janine up in her arms there on the porch and whispered into her ear, "I think it's going to snow today."

Janine poured Maxine a mug of coffee and grabbed her a fresh croissant. They sat out on the large porch that overlooked the vibrant ocean beyond and watched as the fresh light of the morning curled itself toward mid-morning. Within the kitchen, Elsa was in full cook mode — but out there on the porch, Maxine and Janine had nothing but the rush of the ocean waves, the fresh salt in the air, and the warm mugs of coffee within their chilly fingers.

"There!" Maxine pointed as the first flecks of snow fluttered down from the grey sky above. "I knew it."

Janine stood and walked toward the edge of the porch. Once there, she stuck her arm out so that her fingers extended. The snowflakes melted against her skin, unprepared for the warmth of her body.

"Martha's Vineyard snow seems so different than city snow," Janine offered.

"Yes. A very different breed," Maxine admitted.

Maxine spoke briefly about the events of the previous days how nourishing it had felt to be at the Katama Lodge, how she spoke with a number of other women going through their own mental collapses, and how she finally had relearned how to get a good night's sleep. "I can't remember the last time I slept all the way through the night," she stated now. "It feels revolutionary that I even managed it."

"The first step is sleep. Second step, everything else in life," Janine countered.

"I'm a bit nervous about being around your entire family," Maxine admitted tentatively. "But I talked to Nancy about it the other day at the Lodge. She said you've all been through so much over the past few months— that I shouldn't worry." Her smile ached with her fear.

"All we're doing today is sitting around with people we love, despite everything, and eating till we can't eat anymore," Janine said firmly. "No reason to make anything more complicated than it has to be. Okay?"

Maxine nodded as her eyes brimmed with tears she wouldn't let fall. "Okay."

Back inside, Elsa instructed Maxine and Janine to set the table. Maggie and Alyssa were in the living room, clearing the wine glasses of smudges with little towels. Janine had never seen her daughters do much of anything housework-wise. There they sat, like two women from any other era, chatting and gossiping and performing duties that would make the rest of their family's time just the slightest bit brighter. It warmed her heart to watch them.

Henry arrived around twelve-thirty. He was jet-lagged and groggy, but he'd brought with him a few bottles of port from Portugal, along with Portuguese snacks and desserts for everyone to try. Elsa arched an eyebrow ruefully and asked, "Are you suggesting that we don't have everything covered? Because we have everything covered."

"Actually, we have enough food to feed an entire college football team after game day," Alyssa called from the living room.

"Don't listen to any of them," Janine remarked with a laugh. She wrapped her arms around Henry and exhaled into him. "I'm so glad you're here. I'm so glad you're not in China. I don't know if I can even express how glad I am that you're not in China."

"And miss all this?" Henry replied as he gestured toward the dining room table, which was already stuffed to the brim with holiday food. "I wouldn't have. Not for the world."

Bruce arrived after that. He placed a gentle kiss across Elsa's cheek. Almost immediately, her mood shifted and she relaxed into the beauty of the early afternoon. Mallory rushed off to pick up Elsa's other daughter, Alexie, from the ferry station, and by the time they arrived back, Cole appeared with a new girlfriend in tow. Janine found it very difficult to keep up with who he was dating at any given time and had recently decided to just give up.

A vibrant, bronzed turkey was positioned in the center of the table. The final bowls of stuffing, salad, mashed potatoes, yams, and Brussels sprouts were placed around it. Elsa had decided upon Neal's grandmother's china for the day, and its ornate detail glowed beneath the tiny, glittering lights of the dining room's antique chandelier.

Nancy, Janine, Henry, Maxine, Alyssa, Maggie, Mallory, baby Zachery, Mallory's on-again, off-again fiancé, Lucas, Cole and his girlfriend, Bruce, Elsa, Alexie, Nancy, Carmella, Cody, and toddler Gretchen sat around the over-stuffed table and acknowledged the weight of their gratitude.

Perhaps because of the whirlwind of Janine's previous week, she felt the strength to stand to take on the task of prayer. She couldn't remember a single time she'd prayed at another dinner in all the years she'd known Jack. If prayer had been involved, Jack had always been the one to do it. People had always trusted his voice, leaning into the depth of it, the boom of it. Jack's voice was gone, now. He'd left his wife and his lover and his daughters behind to fend for themselves. In many ways, they were better off.

"Dear Lord," Janine began. "It's Thanksgiving Day today and we here in the Remington-Grimson-Potter house have a great deal to be thankful for. It's been the kind of year you make movies about. In many ways, at various times this year, I know we've all thought that we lost everything. Everything we cared for. Everything we poured ourselves into.

"But in that loss, we've gained so much. After many years of separation, my mother and I have finally found our way back to one another. My beautiful eldest daughter was engaged and then married to the man of her dreams. My newfound step-sisters, Elsa and Carmella, both took on hardships and new eras with finesse and courage I've never seen the likes of before. Henry— a true gift— came into my life and showed me fresh perspectives in a way only a documentary filmmaker ever could. And, of course, we welcome Maxine Aubert into our home and our hearts today and all days as we forge new ground forward and make peace with what has come before. I've always believed that this world could be a compassionate one if only we had the strength to make it so. Thank you, oh Lord, for giving us that strength. Amen."

Across the fifty states of America, families who were able ate themselves to the brink of discomfort, took a small break, and continued on in their journey toward over-stuffing, over-sugaring, over-drinking, and over-laughing. Janine felt cocooned with life and love as they tore through the turkey, munched up the green bean casserole, and erupted with laughter at even the slightest joke. Perhaps the sorrow of losing so much had reminded them of the joys they needed to cling to. Perhaps it made those joys just that much stronger.

After dinner, many of them decided on a little walk along the beach to stretch their legs and find some sort of body comfort again. They wrapped themselves up in thick coats, drew gloves over their fingers, and paraded into the grey light. The water lapped up and left lines of white foam across the sands. They fell into pairs— Maggie and Alyssa, Maxine and Nancy, Janine and Henry, Carmella and Cody. Elsa and Bruce remained back at the house to begin the first round of clean-up, as was Elsa's way.

"I think she found a great partner in Bruce," Nancy announced. "He calms her down and isn't afraid to do the dishes when she demands it."

Carmella laughed outright. "He doesn't seem afraid of her at all, not the way we all were yesterday."

Henry spontaneously dropped down, gripped a flat stone, and swept it out across the waters just beyond. It skipped four times before plunging into the depths.

"I'm impressed, yet again," Janine offered.

Henry laughed. "You're too good to me."

Janine's eyes grew to be the size of orbs. She stopped short so that the others marched around her, swimming in their own separate conversations now.

"You're much too good to me, actually," she told him.

"Agree to disagree, I guess," he returned with a wink.

That night, as people gathered around the fire, or returned to their beds, or piled into their vehicles to return home, Janine found herself out in the grim shadows of the front lawn, gazing into the spectacular eyes of Henry Dawson. Everything in her body ached to be with him fully, for the first time. His keys clanked in his hand as they both drummed up the courage to say what they needed to say.

Finally, he whispered, "Do you want to come home with me?"

Janine wished she could smack herself aside the cheek and demand why she felt like such a foolish teenager. She was reminded of the eighteen-year-old version of herself, who hadn't known what the heck kind of Pandora's box she'd opened upon her answer "yes" to a dinner with a handsome stranger named Jack Potter.

"I'd like that very much," she told him. "Let me just go grab some things and say goodbye."

Alyssa, Maggie, and Nancy had sequestered themselves across the fat-cushioned couch with several photo albums spread out across their legs and enough wine between them to get them through the night. Alyssa wagged an old photo in front of her to get Janine's attention. Janine took it and found herself peering at two wayward teenagers, maybe fourteen or fifteen, both in miniskirts and hoop earrings. The sass this otherworldly Janine and Maxine exuded was almost terrifying in its power.

Maxine hustled around the corner just then and stopped short at the sight of the photo.

"Look at us," Janine breathed.

"We look like we own the world," Maxine added.

"Maybe we did."

Maxine's smile was electric, even in its sorrow and heavy nostalgia. "Maybe we really did."

After Janine re-appeared with her coat and her purse, Maxine, Alyssa, Maggie, and Nancy wrapped her up in impossibly tight hugs and set her on her way. Janine felt the warmth of their support as she fell into Henry's arms. This night would almost assuredly lead to an impossibly beautiful future, one of tenderness and light and understanding. It was almost too much to hope for, yet here it was.

# CHAPTER TWENTY-ONE

MAXINE ASKED Janine to head back to the city with her the Saturday after Thanksgiving to retrieve more of her belongings. Janine had set herself up to begin work again the following Wednesday. Henry had a number of emails to write and film segments to edit, and besides, Janine wanted to speak with Jack's lawyer about the specificities of the scholarship program. She agreed to drive Maxine, with one caveat: "You have to play all the music we used to love and nothing else."

When Maxine slipped into the front seat of Janine's vehicle that morning, she said, with excitement, that she'd spent over an hour compiling a playlist for the ride ahead.

"I went all the way down memory lane and back again," she said mischievously. "I hope you enjoy it."

The first song on the playlist— Boyz II Men's, "I'll Make Love to You," made Janine screech with a mix of horror and excitement.

"This is ridiculous," she stated as Maxine hummed the first lines. "Absolutely ridiculous."

"No. What's ridiculous is that time never moved on from 1994," Maxine countered. "We should have always been right there in the coziness of that year, chewing bubble gum and singing this stupid song."

Four and a half hours of nineties nostalgia later, Janine dropped Maxine off at her Upper West Side apartment and then headed downtown to meet with Jack's lawyer for lunch. They met at a swanky little establishment with fifty-dollar lunch plates and large antique mirrors hanging from the walls. Janine remembered a time when she'd thought this sort of lunch was the only lunch you could ever have. Now, she was happy to grab a burger with Henry at the little burger joint near the beach. How times had changed.

After the whirlwind lunch, during which Janine nailed down the initial legalities of the scholarship program (and the lawyer occasionally asked, "Are you really sure you want to do this?"), Janine found herself on the street corner with a bit of time to kill. Maxine required another few hours at her apartment before they'd agreed to meet for another round of reminiscing.

A flower shop beckoned to Janine. Its flurry of fall colors ruffled across the large window while mums dotted the exterior, lying in wait. Jack had never been particularly keen on buying flowers, at least not in the previous twenty-some years. He'd met her twice with roses, which Janine had thought was romantic at the time but now felt was just the easiest option. If Henry bought her flowers, she sensed he would really consider what she might want, outside the bounds of what was considered "appropriate." This was just his way.

Janine purchased a single sunflower from the flower shop owner and carried it with her, twirling it between her fingers as she went. She wasn't far from her destination, but with each step, she soaked up the energy of a city she'd once thought was the very entrance of the universe. Smells swirled around her: baking bagels, fried foods, roasted coffee beans, the trains, and the exhaust from the vehicles. The people seemed chaotic and funny and gritty in ways she could have spoken about but hadn't remembered fully, especially not after her decades in the Upper West Side, being taken by a driver from location to location. She'd lost something when she'd gained in that life. Maybe she could have a bit of it back, even as she fell deeper into her Vineyard world.

The cemetery they'd buried Jack in was the same cemetery where a number of generations of Potters had been buried. They'd positioned Jack alongside his parents, very near to his grandparents, two rows away from his great and great-great-grandparents. Theirs was a family affair of copious earnings. Now, they were all dead, with no one around to taste a single piece of caviar.

As Jack had only recently died, they hadn't yet finished the gravestone. Jack remained an unmarked space, a slab where grass hadn't yet found it within itself to grow. Janine knelt down at the base of this grass and positioned the sunflower directly in the center of the soil.

"I never imagined I would come to see you like this," Janine began to speak in a soft voice. "I thought my hatred for you and what you did to our family would keep me away forever. But I feel differently now. I feel that you and I were uniquely flawed people, from uniquely flawed and complicated pasts, who came together for a portion of time and actually found happiness, if only briefly. I want to thank you for those happy years before we found the darkness. I want to thank you for giving me two of the most beautiful daughters a woman could ask for. I want to thank you for making me feel that things were possible— that I could be a wife and a mother and a high-society woman, to boot. You gave me so much. And I hope you know that I gave you all I could in return. I love you, Jack. In my own silly way, and for my own silly reasons that no one could possibly understand, I will always love you. But that's the thing about love, isn't it? We just can't help it."

Janine pressed her lips against the tips of her fingers and then pressed those fingers against the soil. It was one final kiss. Maybe she and the girls would return here in the spring when the gravestone had been laid. The etching of his name, Jack Potter, would maybe feel too final. Just now, it was as though he lived in the air and the trees and the grass of this ornate, centuries-old cemetery. He was a part of New York City history, now, just as he'd always planned to be.

Maxine and Janine met hours later at The Scrapyard. They held hands just outside, both acknowledging that they still felt this strange urge to reach for their fake IDs.

"Even at forty-three, I still feel like we're breaking the law," Janine admitted.

When they entered, TLC's 1995 hit, "Waterfalls," played on the speakers as though they'd stepped through a different era of time. And funnily enough, a very familiar man appeared over the counter, his arms extended out across the bar as he took in the full view of them.

"Don't tell me," Reggie, the old bartender, now-owner of The

Scrapyard, boomed. "Am I in for some serious trouble now, or what?"

---

# OTHER BOOKS BY KATIE

---

The Vineyard Sunset Series

Sisters of Edgartown Series

Secrets of Mackinac Island Series

A Katama Bay Series

Mount Desert Island Series

Made in the USA
Monee, IL
30 October 2021

81100747R00108